T0066777

Memories of a Disbarred Immigration Lawyer

Memories of a Disbarred Immigration Lawyer

The Statute of Liberty Points East

CLEMENTE CRUZ

Balboa Press books may be ordered through booksellers or by contacting:

Balboa Press
A Division of Hay House
1663 Liberty Drive
Bloomington, IN 47403
www.balboapress.com
1 (877) 407-4847

Print information available on the last page.

ISBN: 978-1-5043-2949-1 (sc)
ISBN: 978-1-5043-2950-7 (e)

Balboa Press rev. date: 4/15/2015

Introduction

Due to the immigration sentiment prevailing in our country today, I thought it may be of some interest as to how it is or was to be an immigration lawyer in Ashtown, IA. I, Clemente Cruz, practiced immigration law from approximately 1991 to 2003-04. I was interested in representing the under and unrepresented. When Legal Aide did not hire me, me, like other unemployed attorneys, hung out our shingle to find food and shelter. As an American born with Mexican ancestors, born in Ashtown, IA in 1957, I encountered racism in many forms and situations, but also was the recipient of Affirmative Action. Totally assimilated and little to no Spanish skills, I took on the duty of protecting and defending those who are commonly known as illegal aliens. Well, I wanted to represent the unrepresented, so there I was. I often wondered, am I breaking the law by aiding and abetting these people? Of course, there is a law that prohibited me or anyone from doing that, but I guess in my case, no. Although my clients were and are often considered criminals, they are not. In this country criminal violators are afforded attorneys according to our Constitution. Illegal immigrants are not criminal offenders by legal definition, but instead are civilly liable for crossing a line in the dirt or passing the line in the Rio Grande River. That way our government can ignore our Constitution and not give them the rights persons within the U.S. boundaries are afforded. How convenient. Can you imagine the outcry by the public if we actually followed our Constitution, and if we gave them our legal benefits paid by taxpayers for normal criminals? Where are the strict constitutionalists now?

I grew up most of my childhood in the South Ashtown and witnesses segregation first hand, until 1965 when the Projects became desegregated. I was around nine when I decided to become a lawyer. It took a while. I graduated from Compton Law School, in Ashtown, IA when I was in my thirties. This story is my efforts to help the unrepresented and how good deeds are often punished. It has some procedural and substantive legal explanations that are needed to explain my method of madness.

CHAPTER ONE

Background

Just a little chronological background. American, with Mexican ancestors born in Ashtown, IA, in the fifties. Farmland, heartland of America, bread basket of America, and the list goes on. From my understanding my mother divorced while pregnant with me. I was named after my Uncle who died in WWII. So my mom who had six children was struggling and we ended up living in the Projects. She remarried my step-dad when I was around nine and we moved North. My parents spoke English and I never realized I was different from anybody. My first realization of being a Mexican, which was kind of weird to me, was in a psychology class when I was 12 years old. There was a survey in the class of all races and levels of prejudice. It went from one, marrying the person, two, being friends, three, have for neighbors, four, it's okay if they live in the city, then five don't want them around and six, of course, exterminating them. Mexicans didn't get even one or two, but thank God that there were no people giving me a six. I left class feeling depressed and alienated, I didn't even know I was Mexican.

I was named after my Uncle who died on DDay and my brother was killed in Viet Nam. How much blood does my family have to shed to be accepted? I moved to the Southwest for a bit and saw a lot of Mexicans, but I just didn't fit in. They all stuck together but I had friends that were white, black and whatever. I knew nothing of Mexican pride and thought it was kind of silly. Plus, I figured we're in America so why even know Spanish? Of course, now you have to know Spanish to live in the United States. That was supposed to be funny. Moved back to crazy, cold North and was the only Mexican that graduated from the class of around 500 at High School.

Finding a girlfriend was somewhat difficult because many girls I dated, their fathers told them no or just get away from me. Some of them listened to their fathers and thankfully, most at them thought for themselves. I had no friends really, except for some misfits, here and there. But I knew I was a good student because I got awards in Spanish and Geometry. Plus, I came in second place in the State High School Chess Championship. Anyway, when I graduated from high school in North I moved back to Ashland to work in the packinghouses. But I still wanted to be a lawyer so I started taking college courses before I turned 18. I worked the second shift and went to college during the day. I did not know about scholarships or financial aid so I just paid out of my work money.

In High School, when I told my counselor I wanted to be a lawyer, he told me I would be better in construction or factory work. Racist? Maybe, I did have a C average. Nonetheless, a little encouragement would have been nice. Despite my counselor's advice, I signed up for some classes at the University of Nantucket in Ashland (UNA) that summer before I turned eighteen. No one in my family had graduated from college, although I had a sister who attended Sunny Land College in Stockyard City, Iowa, but eventually quit because she got married. The point is that I had little to no guidance on what to do. As stated, I paid for my classes for about a year, until a friend of mine told me she was going to (UNA) to apply for a scholarship. Later I found out it was called a Goodyear Scholarship, which was started by Senator Goodyear from the States' Legislature. At first, I thought it might be from the tire company. While waiting for my friend to fill out the papers for the scholarship, one of the professors in the program told me I might as well fill it out too since I was there. Ironically, my friend did not get the scholarship, but I did. It was a scholarship based on financial need, which basically meant minorities and poor whites. It was composed of about one-third Hispanics, one-third black and one-third whites and a few Native Americans. I probably also got the scholarship due to the fact that I had a 4.0 G.P.A. from the classes I had previously paid for. Anyway, I assume I benefited from the scholarship through affirmative action the same way the poor white and the black students did. Having the benefit of living on military bases, being fully assimilated, young and ignorant, I never really got into the politics of the civil rights movement. I just figured I was American and Americans are every race, so what is the problem? Of course, college exposed me to a lot about race relations, so on and so forth, so as a college kid I thought there is nothing wrong with one being proud of one's race and I participated in the Chicano Movement. You know, we are products of our history. Once you start studying history and you see how we got where we are, one starts to get concerned about history repeating itself and we have an obligation that we uphold -- the American notion that we are all equal. For example, Raymond Rodriquez explains in his book, "Decade of Betrayal," how an estimated 1 million Mexicans and Mexican-Americans were deported or scared into leaving their homes because the United States government thought that would improve the economy during the Great Depression. In the place of justice, freedom, and the pursuit of happiness, those of Mexican descent, if they were citizens or not, got deported, and approximately 60% were U.S. citizens! Government officials rounded up Mexican looking people and their families, in dance halls, stores, hospitals, theaters and parks, off the streets, and loaded them in vans and trains and dumped them into Mexico. Enough, I'm feeling sick.

After a couple years in college, I met a young lady who later became my wife. I was so distracted with her (I was nineteen) and got my priorities mixed up and my grades began to suffer. Not bad, just not straight A's and this is not what I wanted with law school in mind. So I dropped out of school with the idea of returning some day, got married and became an electrician. After dropping out of school and adapting to a new lifestyle and responsibilities, it was hard to return to school. Finally in 1988, I registered at a University in Eddy, Texas, by the Mexican border to give it another try. My ex-wife and I were living in my parent's apartment in Patty, Texas, (close to Eddy) and due to some family problems we had to leave. We went back to UNA and the Goodyear Scholarship Program fortunately let me back on the scholarship. While back at school, I again joined some of the Hispanic clubs, or I think they were called Latino then, and joined the pre-law club, Amnesty International, chess club and a fraternity. I became aware of the international human rights violations, how to try to become a better Mexican-American and how to get into law school. Anyway, I graduated with 3.4 average, applied to law schools, got my reference letters and prepared for the LSAT (Law School Admissions Test). My first attempt at the LSAT was not good. It was below average. I never drank coffee and for some strange reason I drank a cup of coffee before the LSAT thinking it might sharpen my thinking. Instead, it gave me one of those headaches where you know if you could just throw up you would feel better. Needless to say, I took it again, without coffee, did better than average, which made me average because with the LSAT, back then anyway, they averaged your test scores. Wow, I was an average potential law student. I guess Harvard was out of the question.

Anyway, not knowing where I was going to law school, I signed up for a program called CLEO (Council on Legal Educational Opportunities), which I was accepted to and spent the Summer of 1991 in Missouri, (the show-me state) at a minority based law school boot camp. It was primarily minorities and some white students who had not been accepted into law school. It was to shore up their resumes and law schools came to the program near its end to interview potential law students. Fortunately, right before CLEO started, I went to Compton Law School for a full ride scholarship I had applied for. There were six scholarships with one hundred and twenty applicants. It was as if fate arrived when Senior law student, Jamie Sanrio, was on the interview committee who lived the same pace I lived down in Texas, in the little town called Patty, by Eddy, Texas. He was instrumental in me obtaining the Scholarship that was provided by Compton. Did affirmative action help me? Yes, it gave me the opportunity to succeed by working hard and playing by the rules. Did affirmative action help my get my G.P.A, my sufficiency on the LSAT, graduation from law school and passing the Bar Exam? No, but it did give me the opportunity to prove myself.

My first year at Compton was hard despite my CLEO training. The saying was 65 to stay alive. I lived by getting a 65 average and not committing suicide. Law school was somewhat of a humbling experience after being on top as an undergrad. I attended both summer sessions between by first and second years at Compton, so by time my third year arrived, I had most the credits I needed to graduate. My resume at Compton was full of extra curricular activities.

My first year consisted primarily of studying, worrying, and trying to catch my breath most of the time. However, I did meet an immigration lawyer, Jim Jones, who took me under his wing and started showing me the ropes. After my first year, I started working for him, primarily writing appellate briefs to the BIA (Board of Immigration Appeals). Most of them were about asylum. Also after my first year, during the summer, a classmate of mine, Jim Fellows and I started investigating law school clinics around the country. We compiled research and composed a proposal to the Compton Law School faculty and Dean to have one at Compton. Thankfully, they started it and Jim and I were in the first class during our third year in the clinic. We also started a group on campus called the Public Interest Law Forum, which specialized in poverty law. The group still exists to my knowledge. My second year of law school was more of the same. I was now Vice-president of the Latino Law Student Association, promoted from secretary, and eventually became President my third year. I was deeply influenced by a transfer student, Flor Chavez, from Santa Clara Law School from California who was energetic and a visionary. We started a mentor program with a High School (a school with the most Latinos) to help high school Hispanic students learn about college and trying to steer them in the right direction. We also started an internship at the local Legal Aide. We coordinated with the Compton Campus wide Latino group to sponsor events and awareness. I was awarded a campus wide award called the Father Scholmer Award at a banquet. It was obviously named after Father Scholmer, who was a Priest who did lots of community work and volunteerism without the need of recognition. It also put me on the Wall of Distinction at the Campus Student Center. I am not writing this to show I love myself and that others should love me; I just want the reader(s) to know I had good motives to help the under-represented and was fortunate enough to set some things in motion. I was also awarded the highest grade award for my immigration law class in my third year at Compton.

Lastly, I should tell about my families (the Cruz side on my mom's side) migration to the United States. My grandfather, Clemente Cruz, came here from Guadalajara, Mexico around the turn of the twentieth century. He moved to Stockyard City, Iowa. He worked in the Packing House for around thirty years and had thirteen children. Well, he was Catholic. My mom was born around 1925 and eventually moved to Ashtown, where I was born as a natural born citizen, thank God.

CHAPTER TWO

The Beginning Years

After many job searches and some interviews with no success, I turned to Jim, who told me he could take me in for $10.00 an hour. That was more than the six dollars I got from him as a law clerk. I needed a law related job and took it. I was working around 80 hours a week, so I was still able to afford an apartment and a car, although I did not have a lot of time to enjoy them. Before Jim added me to his staff, he had hired another lawyer, Pauly May. The office was set up to where Jim did the immigration law, Pauly would do divorce and personal injury and I would do employment law. Being straight out of law school with little to no experience than my employment law class at Compton, I blundered my way though it my first year. As I found out, employment law encompasses workers' compensation, social security issues, job injuries, wages, OSHA, etc.... I saw many undocumented workers taken advantage of because they had no work permit, just false papers. The employers knew this. Consequently, they knew they could pretty much use, abuse and throw away their people, my clients. I won a few cases but saw the advantage employers had dealing with these workers, who had deportation hanging over their heads. There are a lot of stories I could say about these obvious abuses, but what I learned is that if you work in the United States without a work permit or legal status, you are not afforded the protection of our laws, which includes wages, safety, Social Security benefits, benefits in general, or any type of retirement or pension. As a lawyer searching for justice for some of the most misrepresented people in society, I felt helpless to the corporate and employers' tactics against these workers. In a recent conversation with an ICE (Immigration and Custom Enforcement) agent, I told him that the immigrants are not causing wages to fall. It is the employers who pay them that are suppressing the wages. They dictate the wages, not the immigrants. I asked him why isn't there more emphasis on going after employers who hire these workers? He told me that the procedure and red tape in the agency (DHS-Department of Homeland Security) was so burdensome that it was almost impossible to implement the law against the employers. It is so strange that the new immigrants are blamed for lowering wages. It is not like they tell employers, "Pay me little to nothing," they just feel fortunate to take crumbs, knowing they have no say, especially when deportation is hanging over their heads.

During my year as an "employment lawyer", I was also helping Jim with his immigration cases. I basically did everything from consultations to representing them at court. I won my first asylum case. One I did for Jim. That was a big accomplishment especially because Jim had only won one asylum case in the last three years. In defense to

Jim and myself, taking a case to trial in immigration is like taking a case that is already lost.

As much as I wanted to stay away from substantive and procedural legal borishism, I should explain the procedural aspect of asylum law. It is different from other areas of relief for an immigrant. But before I go any further, I should state that the word "immigrant" is actually a legal term meaning a person who is not a USC (United States Citizen), who has legal status to stay here from some type of visa or other legal vehicle. I am using immigrant in the vernacular as a person who lives on earth who travels from one region to another region despite the country of destination's definition or border. One who files for asylum, in Nebraska and Iowa, anyway, has to file the application (I-589), which goes to the Lincoln Service Center. Lincoln will send out the notices to the applicant of receipt and put on the receipt the date it was received, which is important because if the application is not adjudicated by the IJ (Immigration Judge) by 150 days, the applicant is eligible for a work permit. In the 1994-95, one could get a work permit immediately, but that changed around 1996-97 when they changed the law to stop immigrants from filing applications to receive work permits. Anyway, the district office gets a copy from Lincoln that the application was received by Lincoln and coordinates with the Asylum Office in Chicago, which sets an appointment for an interview with the applicant. Everyone receives notice for these interviews, the client, their attorney, if they have one, and the District office. The client goes to the interview and is examined by an asylum officer who determines if the claim merits permanent residency. If not, the case is sent to the IJ(Immigration Judge), who sets a Master

Calendar hearing (basically the same as an arraignment in the criminal court), where the immigrant states what form of relief they want. In these cases, normally asylum, unless they have other forms of relief, (which are too exhaustive to get into here). Are you still following me or are your eyes starting to get a glaze over them with a blank stare? They (attorneys) admit that immigration law is the most difficult area to practice other than the tax code. Anyway, my original point is that when immigration lawyers get asylum cases, they get cases that have already lost at the administrative level; consequently, we are defending a lost or losing case. It is probably like public defenders who defend people with losing cases. One gets used to losing except in those rare moments when the improbable win happens. Being a new, optimistic, naive lawyer, I took every case seriously with the intention to win. Just like taking a final exam in school, you do not have test anxiety if you are prepared. I had read every book, manual and case dealing with asylum to feel like I would win every case or if I did not, it was not for lack of preparation. I will comment more in the procedure and substantive law concerning asylum later.

After my first year of "employment lawyer" and quasi immigration lawyer (doing Jim's cases), I asked Jim if I could get some of my own immigration clients. He agreed and gave me some expenses to pay along with my independence. Things were moving fast and slow at the same time. For example, after I had been in the office for a few months, Jim let me answer an asylum question on the phone. When he handed the phone to me, my hand was shaking along with my voice as I carefully and hopefully accurately answered the question. It was kind of one of those times when you realize what you are doing and its consequences. As a lawyer, you should be accurate and competent because you basically have these peoples' lives or at least their near future in your hands. It is frightening at first, but like most things and years later, I could answer most questions in my sleep.

Getting my own clients around allowed me to build my clientele. That was good, but what I did not know was that representing immigrants was so emotionally draining. I saw so many families getting torn apart. Children crying, parents crying, siblings crying, spouses crying, and I had to be strong or at least be able to choke out, "I did the best I could do and I'll keep trying to help," but in a lot of cases, I had to tell my clients that's all I could do, then go in my office and cry too. I got so sick of the government spouting out that we are a country of "family values" that I could scream. In my second year of representing my clients, I was getting more successful with my cases and crying less. I kept hearing from other lawyers that you have to grow another layer of skin or get a skin of leather. What actually happened is that I just got numb, probably like an accident investigator who gets used to seeing dead bodies after hundreds of accidents. I was still winning cases enough to get attention from other immigrants. Immigrants are generally well connected; consequently, I was getting cases primarily from word of mouth. Ethically, lawyers are suppose to find out if a potential client has another lawyer in their consultations. If so, the lawyer is supposed to stop talking to them unless they fire (discharge) their present attorney. I found myself in a precarious situation when some of Jim's clients wanted me to represent them. Keeping the teaching of ethics in mind, I would sometimes find out that the people I was talking to had Jim as their lawyer. I told them I could not represent them at that point unless they wanted to discharge Jim. I asked a few times if that was what they really wanted to do because I did not want Jim to be upset with me. Jim was a friend and colleague of mine and had helped me, but I regrettably went to his office, told him the circumstances and asked for his client's file. After doing that a few times, Jim told me I had to leave and gave me a few days to do so.

CHAPTER THREE

The Middle Years

The immigrant population was growing at this time and there were few immigration lawyers, maybe five or six that I knew of. Some of those immigration lawyers only did employment based law like HB1s or visas for executive and managerial like the Ls and Ms. The visas available are like alphabet soup. I did not deal with those cases. I was strictly deportation defense with few tools to use as forms of relief from deportation. The term deportation has been changed to removal which is basically the same thing. The only difference is that before they had deportation and exclusion, which is the same as deportation, except the person is apprehended at the border. Those terms consolidated became removal. Like most areas of law, it is best to specialize. With immigration one has to find a specialty within the specialty of immigration law, to be competent. Anyway, due to the fact that few lawyers practiced deportation defense, I was swamped. I found an office that was next to the district immigration office and there were few dull moments. By now, I was not only reading the books, manuals and case law, I was now subscribing to magazines, listening to immigration law tapes whenever I drove, and attending any and all immigration conferences. I was trying to make myself a walking, talking and breathing immigration machine. I was still being relatively successful with my cases so my clientele escalated to unanticipated proportions.

I am not sure if you are aware of the geography of Nebraska and Iowa, but that was the prevailing immigration district with the main INS (Immigration and Naturalization Service, now DHS-Department of Homeland Security) office in Chicago. Consequently, my clients could end up driving 300 or 400 miles. I saw that as a logistical problem because people who potentially had forms of relief from deportation could not drive all that way. Consequently, I thought it would be better if I could go to them. It also afforded me to talk to my clients who were in those other cities. I ended up having close to ten offices where I would meet my current clients and have consultations. First, I started to go to Northern Iowa about a hundred miles away. There is a regulation from the Federal Register (a manual explaining interpretation of laws, by government agencies) that allows an accredited person (not lawyers) to represent immigrants in Federal Court, before the IJ and probably the BIA, too. I informed the agency I was visiting to see clients about the BIA accreditation program. I noticed after a while that my clientele was shrinking there and they finally told me that one of their staff members got accreditation. I think they were afraid of offending me, but I was happy. There were more immigrants than I could help and any other help was appreciated. They probably thought they were taking my clientele, but there were not enough lawyers to handle all the people anyway. This brings up the subject of notorios. Notorios are notary publics. In Mexico and maybe other Latin American countries, notorios act as lawyers; consequently, many of the immigrants think that notiorios are as good as lawyers here. Of course, that is not true. What was good about notorios in Nebraska and Iowa is that there were not enough lawyers to handle all the clientele. What was bad about notorios was that sometimes they gave bad advice or hold themselves out as lawyers, then take advantage of immigrants. In our district anyway, they were generally well intended persons who wanted to help immigrants. The biggest complaint of most immigration lawyers was that they were practicing law without a license. That argument was without much teeth though because they primarily filled out immigration forms, took passport pictures, interpreted and translated documents. Anyone can fill out a form legally because immigration forms generally have a section on the forms indicating who filled out the form other than the applicant, which they are required to sign. As stated, I welcomed them as well intended persons who wanted to help. I had more clients than I knew what to do with, so I never felt any competition with them and encouraged the ones I dealt with to get accredited.

The more I dealt with INS/DHS, the more I realized the whole notion behind the anti-immigrants sentiment that prevails. First, the primary INA (Immigration and Naturalization Act) was enacted in the fifties, which means segregation, Jim Crow laws, rampant discrimination and the visa bulletin. The visa bulletin is basically a chart of categories, quotas, and priority dates (date the agency gets an applications) where countries like Mexico, China, Philippines, India, and the Dominic Republic are more harshly penalized. Does anyone see a certain pattern and mindset, or is just me?

Thoughtful analysis is not necessary to see that certain countries have quotas in the equation where the priority date is necessary to get the the green card, so they can prepare for the citizenship test to be eligible to actually become a citizen. It reminds me of when affirmative action started. Everyone was against quotas because they are discriminatory. I could go into further discussion as to why aren't there any European countries on the list? But as I heard before, "these truths are self evident." Quotas in any capacity are discriminatory. Lastly, the Statute of Liberty does face East to Europe, not South to Mexico. It reads something like, "The air-bridged harbor that twin cities frame. Keep, ancient lands, your storied pomp!" cries she with silent lips. "Give me your tired, your poor, your huddled masses yearning to breathe free, the wretched refuse of your teeming shore. Send these, the homeless, tempest-tossed to me, I lift my lamp beside the golden door!" Most of us forgot to look at the footnote on the bottom which reads, "Except Mexicans." Lastly, sorry for those who do not want this land of immigrants to stay a land of immigrants. More than half of us would be deported if we had to pass the citizenship test to be U.S. Citizens.

> As I told my clients, your rights stop at the border. I believe that there is a god-given right to travel. I am not saying that we should not have some criteria for people coming into the United States like people who are criminals or with contagious

> diseases, but it should not be country specific. However, we have jails and hospitals for them too. We shouldn't be like Europe was when their migration started, when they use to empty out their prisons and send them here. As Joyce Bryant points out in her article "Immigration in America."
>
> Some colonists sought adventure in America. Others fled religious persecution. **Many** were convicts transported from English jails. *But most immigrants by far hoped for economic opportunity.* Source: The World Book Encyclopedia, Volume 10, Page 82).
>
> As pointed out in this article, most immigrants came here for economic opportunities. As a historian, political scientist, and lawyer, I felt that our neighbors from the south should also be afforded the same opportunities as our previous immigrants. That notion is what got me in trouble later. Is it safe to say the more things change the more they stay the same?

And what is the phase "wetback" about? They only crossed a river (sometimes flew into the U.S.) not the whole entire ocean. Should the Europeans be called "waterlogged" and the ships that brought them be called cartel (they did send their criminals here) coyote boats with boat people. I'm included. Mexicans are actually Spanish Europeans who mixed with this continent's indigenous Natives. In my case the Aztec Indian Tribe. Immigration should be whoever is first in line should be served first. That would be fair. I forgot. The main thing I heard in law school, over and over again, was there is fairness, and than there is the law. We were not allowed to use the word fair, which in turn means no justice. Our laws are usually a generation or two behind us, anyway. Nonetheless, just because our laws are not fair does not mean that we should not strive to make them so.

My hatred was growing against the Brown Shirt Gestapo tactics that INS/DHS used against Mexicans and others. For example, I had a client who had three U.S.C. children and had lived here for over fifteen years that called me while in detention. A perfect candidate for Cancellation of Removal (COR). To be eligible for COR, one had to be here ten years, have a spouse, parent, or child(ren) that are either a permanent resident or U.S.C. and it would be a extreme hardship if they are deported, and are of good moral character (no felonies or other crimes that could rise to the term by INS/DHS called an "aggravated felony.)" Anyway, I told her not to sign anything or say anything. Just tell them you want to talk to your lawyer. That is what I told all my clients. But she told me as many other clients told me. She got intimidated by Deportation (now ICE) who told her that her lawyer could not do anything except take her money and then made her sign deportation papers in English that she was not even sure what it was that she signed. I also heard this from other lawyers.

INS/DHS had a few liaison meetings where the local immigration lawyers could ask questions to ICE, District Council - Charlie Brown, and Linux Hoss- District Director. Of course, they denied any such actions against our clients who were subjected to their initial detentions. They should have called them *Lie*ason meetings instead of liaison meetings. We also had an issue with the filing of CORs. Many of us had clients that were eligible for the form of relief, but INS/DHS would not adjudicate them; consequently, delaying an eligible immigrant an opportunity to become a permanent resident. So they told us that they would start adjudication of them, which never happened. It was somewhat of a risk to submit the applications because, as the name implies, it is an attempt to cancel one's deportation/ removal. So first the client has to turn themselves in, bond out, then go before the Immigration Judge (IJ). They were difficult cases because they were very labor intensive and paper heavy. We had to first show they were here at least ten years with various documents (receipts, tax receipts, school records, etc. . . . .). Then they had to go through a criminal check which was done, back then anyway, with fingerprints. They also had to have good moral character, which basically means a good record. Lastly, and maybe most importantly, they had to show extreme hardship to their qualifying family member. Extreme hardship is somewhat a subjective criteria, which means it was worse than just a hardship; for example, it has to be worse than just leaving ones' children here alone and them losing their financial support from the applicant. Can you imagine? They changed the law around 1996-97 when it was formally called Suspension of Deportation (SOD). SOD was primarily the same as COR, except it changed seven years to ten and changed hardship to extreme hardship. Although, I haven't read the legislative history (if it even explains the change) the change corresponds with the Legalization Act (Amnesty) that President Reagan implemented, which was enacted in 1989. 1996 is seven years away from 1989. I suspect the change was to stop any Mexicans who had not qualified from Amnesty to be eligible for SOD, so they changed it to ten years. It would also stop any qualifying immigrants from trying to get SOD for another three years and make it more difficult. I could really see how easy it was for a group of people to hate another group. Anyway, it was somewhat ironic when our clients would go into the District Office to turn themselves in so they could file their COR, and were turned away. Can you imagine our then legal ancestors going through this to live here legally, now? Wow!

What was so good and important about COR is that the client/applicant/petitioner can present their case in front of the IJ. This affords the immigrant to also present any other applications (forms of relief) before the IJ. For future reference, it is legal and not unethical to do this in immigration law. Actually it's better. Some practitioners use this "shot gun approach." It makes sense and is beneficial to one's clients. This is similar to asylum in that if it denied at the administrative level, it is mandatory to go to trial, which is called the Individual Hearing in immigration. This is important to clients/immigrants who are married to U.S.C.s because in 1996-97, the law was changed to where a U.S.C., was once able to adjust their status to "a conditional permanent resident" (CPR) without having to go to ones' home country. After 1997, April 15, I believe, if a U.S.C. married an immigrant, the immigrant would have to go to their home country, that is with the qualification that if a person's I-130 had its priority date before April 15, 1997. The new procedure of the spouse of a U.S.C. going to their home country is called Consular Processing, because they have to go to the U.S. Consulate in their home country to have their I-485 (adjustment to permanent residency) adjudicated instead of having it done administratively in the U.S. That was one advantage of applying for asylum - since an Individual Hearing was mandatory, one could present other forms of relief and withdraw the asylum application. Henceforth, the asylum application could act as a vehicle to bypass Consulate Processing as a legal procedural tactic. They taught us in law school that you need to use all your tools to represent your clients zealously. For example, if the facts are bad, argue the law; if the law is bad, argue the facts; if those are bad, argue public policy and I would add, pull any and all tools out to complete a job, just like when I did construction. As a caveat, one cannot do this when you represent the lowest of the low in our society. If you find legal advantages (loopholes) or use all your tools in corporate America, you are a hero; if you want to help those on the bottom of the totem pole, watch out. Can you imagine our ancestors having to go through this to be legally here? Our ancestors invaded and stoled this land from natives, claiming God brought us here to civilize the natives through "Manifest Destiny." I'm not saying this to be critical, but something we can learn from. I don't think we really have to worry about the new immigrants taking over through any aggressive doctrine, especially with the current police, government and military lock down.

Before I go any further I should go through the administrative procedure concerning obtaining conditional permanent residency through marriage to a U.S.C. Initially, if a U.S.C. married an immigrant, the process was rather simple. The U.S.C. went and got the forms I-130 and I-485. The I-130 is the Alien Relative Petition. Once that is received at the Nebraska Service Center, in this region, it is stamped with the date received, which is the priority date. The priority dates correspond with the Visa Bulletin dictating when one can adjust their status with the I-485, the Petition to Adjustment of Status Application. Basically, it takes these two applications to get permanent residency (green card). The I-130 and the I-485. If a U.S.C. marries an immigrant, their initial status is called a CPR (conditional permanent resident) in order to prevent "sham marriages." You know, where an immigrant marries just for their green card. Now the immigrant is a CPR for two years of marriage, then is eligible for permanent residency. When the CPR is eligible to get their permanent residency, it is usually the same time that the agency calls the couple in for an interview. You have heard of these interviews before where the examining officer asks questions like, where is the light switch in the hallway and/or what side of the bed do you sleep on, etc. . . .? This is basically to ensure it is not a sham marriage. There are also sham divorces. Due to the categories for family based visas, based on unmarried and married family members, I had heard of immigrants getting divorced in order to make their priority date sooner. Our current immigration system encourages family breakups. Good thing our ancestors got to skip these steps. But it's legal! Well, so was the guillotine!

Before I go off onto another tangent, my point about asylum cases and COR affords a marriage to be adjudicated before an IJ, because it is mandatory for asylum and COR cases to go to court to get adjudicated. However, once a married couple gets in front of an IJ, they can adjudicate their I-130 or I-485 avoiding Consular Processing, regardless of their priority date.

Sorry, if this is confusing, but these factors were important in my plan to help my clients stay here in the most efficient, timely manner. If I could get my clients to go to court instead of having their cases adjudicated by the agency, it would spare the newlyweds from going to the immigrant's home country. But why keep things simple like our ancestors had it? Yes, I'm confused to! It couldn't be to much government, racism, discrimination, hate, fear, avoiding strange people, or part of a conservative agenda? No, nothing like that!

One thing that bothered me was that Deport/ICE always got busier during the Holiday Season. I could not figure it out. Why would they concentrate on destroying families especially during Christmas? Did they get bonuses and need the extra money during Christmas? Did they have to meet a yearly quota that was not being met during the year? Or were they just mean spirited. Maybe a combination of all those factors. Whatever it was, it did not help me gain a favorable opinion of the agency. Good thing our ancestors who immigrated "legally" didn't have to jump through this hoop too!

What really bothered me about INS/DHS was that they wanted me to join them. I politely declined while thinking, "Why would I go work for the anti-christ?" I know federal workers make good money with great pensions, but I had to look at myself in the mirror. I did not know how any human being could work for them when their main goal was to deport people, destroy families, shatter dreams, and stomp on human kind! Even most of the IJs were former government immigration lawyers. Consequently, when I was in court, it was like me against two government lawyers. The

IJs came into their judge-ships with a propensity to deport. To make matters even worse, if possible, the immigration judges are hired by the Department of Injustice and are bound by them because they are their client. How could a judge be impartial? Furthermore, the government attorneys are also hired by the Department of Injustice. I'll let you do the math. I am glad that they changed the name to Department of Homeland Security instead of Immigration and Naturalization Service because there was not much "service" to speak of.

INS did ask me if I was willing to represent any clients pro bono (free). I told them I would, even though at the time my clients owed me hundreds of thousands of dollars. INS/DHS never did get a hold of me to represent any of these clients. I hated to ask my clients for money because I knew most of them worked at low paying, labor intensive jobs. I also knew how it was to work at a job where you feel like you got hit by a truck after work, after fifteen years in construction. I did not have the heart to have my clients pay huge retainers like most of the immigration lawyers did. I charged my clients $75.00 a month no matter what I was doing even if I was going to trial, writing a brief, or going with them to INS. Jim had everyone pay $100.00 a month. I think a lot of lawyers did not like the idea that I was charging so little, but I thought it was ridiculous to make people pay thousands of dollars for a retainer when they have families and were working for eight or nine dollars an hour. Jim even told me that I had to charge more to be in step with the other lawyers' fees. What kind of s!@%t was that? It was bad enough that they were being taken advantage of by everyone else. I did not want a part of that. I had another lawyer tell me to stay out of his territory. What's up with that? I had to live with my conscience. Needless to say, I think most lawyers did not like me because of this and there might have been some jealousy too.

Another fallacy I hear is that immigrants do not pay taxes. Most, if not all my clients, had jobs where payroll taxes were taken out. I guess that is okay, but most, if not all my clients were afraid to file taxes for their refund. They figured that the least exposure to the government (that wants to deport them) was wise. I could see their reasoning, but why give the government money that is owed to them? My clients figured because they did not have a correct social security number, they did not want to flag the government of their address. It was safer to let the government have the tax money that was owed. As USA Today reported in 2006:

> Many illegal immigrants pay up at tax time.
> By Travis Loller, Associated Press
>
> NASHVILLE — The tax system collects its due, even from a class of workers with little likelihood of claiming a refund and no hope of drawing a Social Security check. Illegal immigrants are paying taxes to Uncle Sam, experts agree. It is hard to determine because the federal government doesn't fully tally it, but it's around $9,000,000.00 per year

When my clients told me that, I told them to claim their refunds from as far back as they could. Go to H & R Block or wherever and claim their refund that they were entitled to despite their legal status. Most immigrants and maybe even practitioners do not know that the taxes the immigrants pay into the system will count towards their social security retirement in the event they become permanent residents or U.S. Citizens, even if it was not their correct social security number. The immigrants can use the money they put into their fake social security number to calculate their retirement benefits. If they do not file, then they will likely never be able to use the taxes they were entitled to receive through their refund. I have heard contrary studies to what I witnessed here concerning taxes and maybe things were different in other parts of the country, but as far as my clients were concerned, they paid way more than their fair share of taxes.

There is also some type of notion that our neighbors from the South and visa overstayers (whom are actually approximately 60% of the new immigrants) come here for welfare. First off, the other 40% of the people that make it are young and strong. Many of them survived the Arizona dessert. They are more likely candidates for the morgue than social welfare. In the years I practiced immigration law, I never met a client on welfare. Maybe their U.S. citizen child was getting WIC, an education, or medical help, but they are U.S. citizen children. I know our immigrant children attend public school pursuant a Supreme Court decision. "Plyler v. Doe". Now things are getting turned around. If we are a nation of laws and if our highest court in Plyler states all children are entitled a free public education, the fact that all children are entitled to an education should be a moot point. Oh I forgot, we live in a land of selective enforcement. Lets go after the children. I am not even going to go into the health care issue concerning immigrants other than to say we treat our animals better than them.

Maybe someday when the insurance companies, banks, pharmaceutical corporations, wall street and the rich think our country should be healthy, instead of making money off of human misery, we might all have free health care, but that is another book. Lastly, it is shameful that European countries provide health care to their immigrants, while we cannot even fathom helping our immigrants in any positive manner. Good thing our ancestors were not subject to such "legal" conditions.

I thought things were going bad for immigration practitioners before 9/11. Despite that comment, in retrospect, things were not so bad pre-9/11. There was a lot of talk of amnesty before 9/11, especially with President Bush's push to find a pathway for citizenship for the Mexican Nationals and others who were in the U.S. I knew if I could just keep my clients here one way or the other, when the new laws (there were various proposals) were enacted all my clients who were here would be more than likely eligible for the relief. I imagined it would be something to the effect that our new immigrants would have to have clean criminal records (no problem), be here for a number of years, pay any back taxes (or in my clients' cases get their refunds), know basic English, and have ties in the U.S. such as a business, family, property, etc. It may be a surprise to some people (immigrant haters), but the majority of the immigrants have perfectly clean criminal records. It does not take a genius to figure out that if one is in a foreign country that is trying to deport them, that they will lay low and stay out of any trouble. Not to mention, that they have come here to better themselves like all the other immigrants. The only difference is that this country has decided to slam the door on these immigrants. As a person caring for his fellow person, whom are all blessed with God's divinity, with Bush's immigrant agenda, I was a Bush supporter in that area just like I praised Reagan's Amnesty. We should be building bridges not walls!

I was always a little perplexed about why can't we be as helpful to our Southern neighbors as we were to our European brothers. We let our ancestors in with a checkup to see if they had contagious diseases, twenty dollars and an I.D. Now, thousands of dollars to file petitions, thorough medical exams, quotas, fear of deportation, attorney fees, and the list goes on. I also hear about how there are not enough resources and land to take them in. Anyone drive across the Midwest lately, (without falling asleep)? There is more than enough room and resources. Besides that, growth in population self perpetuates development and economic growth. The new immigrants need houses, cars, jobs, create businesses. etc. . . . And if there is not enough room, then this country would have enacted some type of birth control measures limiting the size of families. This country is not worried about population growth, only about what segment of the population that is growing. Which brings me to the Latino birth rate.

Remember when the ancient Aztec and Mayan tribes ruled Central America? Me neither, but they appeared to have had population control in the form of sacrifices. Of course, the idea behind human sacrifices was not for population control, it was to please the gods. However, when the Spanish arrived with their bibles and Catholicism, the people now let go of their former worship ceremonies and practiced the Catholic theology of no birth control or abortions. Voila, last census reports that approximately 85%

of population growth was Latinos and will be the majority population before 2050. Maybe in this case we should thank the Europeans. We are now very fruitful and are probably going to solve the Social Security dilemma, if we can put this youngest portion of our population legal, so they can contribute more into the system. Another argument is that terrorist can come in from the South. Okay, we totally neglect the Canadian border while at the same time, I do not think there is any documented proof of any Mexican terrorists. Although, Fox News (questionable) states, as I paraphrase, "Well, not really Mexican terrorist (although the drug cartels should be classified as such), but other subversives who can get here through Mexico." Okay, make our border look like a fortified prison outpost. Good bye to the "build bridges not walls" saying. Another is that Mexicans bring in drugs, guns and crime. Guns are illegal in Mexico. Ninety percent of the guns (artillery) confiscated in Mexico are from the U.S. I have covered crimes, unless you count the unconstitutional dogma counting civil violations (crossing the border) with criminals who are supposed to be afforded rights, like a lawyer, which is not afforded to our new immigrants. But drugs are the biggest complaint. All I have to say to that is there is no supply without demand. Economics 101. If we Americans stop their insatiable appetite for any foreign substance they can cram into their bodies, there would be no drug supply from Mexico or anywhere else for that matter, except the U. S. pharmaceutical corporations.

As previously mentioned, I have limited Spanish skills. Being a third generation Mexican-American, I only attended Public Schools where English is the prevailing language. My parents both knew Spanish, but did not speak it at home unless they got mad or were saying something they did not want us to understand. Furthermore, my mom had related to me that when she attended school, she was not allowed to speak Spanish and would get into trouble if she did. Consequently, there was no pressure or need to speak Spanish living in the Midwest and I think my mom thought it was more important that we become assimilated until we moved to California when I was around twelve or thirteen. Then my parents tried to encourage me to speak Spanish. By now, being a teenager (knowing everything), I thought as long as I am in the U.S., what do I have to know Spanish for? I never thought I would need it. Now that I was thrust into being an immigration lawyer, it sure could have helped. I had interpreters in my office, because of my lack of Spanish, which did not help me much to learn Spanish. Nevertheless, I did learn a lot of Spanish, but still did not have to practice it due to my interpreters. I had a few Mexican girlfriends who helped me a lot, but with foreign languages you have to practice or you forget. My point is that I depended on my interpreters to accurately tell my clients what I was saying. I did trust them. A lot of my clients came to me because of my name, Clemente Cruz. When they came to my office and learned I did not know Spanish, they usually still trusted me, but some of them left. Sometimes while waiting for the interpreter to come for a consultation, I would try to speak my broken Spanish to them. When they heard how bad my Spanish was, they would try to speak to me in English, which was usually pretty good considering their circumstances. One last point is that while growing up in the Midwest in the 1950s and

60s, our family was maybe one of the ten Mexican families in the area and we all knew each other. While practicing law in the 1990s and early 2000, where I grew up, is now known as Little Mexico.

The practice of law is like most other jobs where you learn what to do. Unfortunately it is often learned by the mistakes you make. I have come to the conclusion that mistakes equal experience if you learn from the mistakes, which means the better you get also probably equates to the many more mistakes you have made from someone inexperienced. Of course, it is better to learn from someone else's mistake, but that is not always possible. Ironically, failure and mistakes makes success. I did make mistakes, which in turn, I thought made me a better lawyer. My biggest complaint is that everything was going too slow. There was only so much I could do. Then it was INS/DHS turn. Waiting on them is like watching paint peel. That was something I had to constantly tell my clients, which was not always satisfactory. Around 1995 or so, I met up with an old friend of mine, who had a bother- in- law who had sold drugs to an undercover officer. He had a lawyer doing his appeal and he wanted to have me do it. I agreed and thought he was going to get the file from his other lawyer and he thought I was going to get it. Needless to say, he called me a day before the appellate brief was due. I tried to get a continuance on the case, but the Nebraska Supreme Court denied it. My client filed a complaint to the Bar and they gave me a private reprimand stating something like, even if I would have filed the brief, the likelihood of its success was minimal to null due to the fact that he sold to an undercover officer. I got another reprimand after an incident with my now ex-wife around 1998. I lied to the police after a heated argument with my wife stating that she attacked me. I admitted I was guilty at court, got a fine for false reporting, and the judge contacted the Bar and they gave me a private reprimand. I also got quite a few complaints from clients complaining that I was neglecting their cases. I explained to the Bar that there was only so much I could do then, that I had to wait for INS/DHS. The Bar realized that I could not control INS/DHS's response time and routinely dismissed the complaints. Another problem our ancestors did not encounter.

What gets me is the United States' arrogance that everyone wants to live here. For some reason, the bureaucrats believe everyone wants to live here despite our declining influence in the world. Furthermore, naturally people feel accepted and closer in their home country. The United States has job opportunities. That is why people come here, not always for the "freedom" and our way of life. I like the Midwest, but I moved South to find a job, but I still would rather be in the Midwest because I was born here and have family here.

The discussion about changing the Fourteenth Amendment about natural born people becoming Citizens is a blatant attack on Mexicans having babies here. I just wish the constitutionalist would figure it out. Are we going to follow the Supreme Law of the Land - the Constitution or not? And then the Arizona style laws. The Constitution says the Federal Government is supposed to control immigration, not the states. What is so hard to figure out? I guess the attack on the dead Constitution has not stopped. You know, we follow it if it meets our needs and otherwise, forget it.

I'm a little disheartened by the attack on certain people. I was named after my Uncle, who died in WWII. My brother died in Viet Nam. Most of my relatives on my mom's side joined the military and fought in every war you can think of, especially because they joined the Marines. A couple of years ago, I was asked for my green card. When is this racial profiling going to stop? Has my family spilled their blood and died in vain? Looks like it. It is sad when all we want to do is contribute to this country, lay our lives down for it, get a little respect, then get kicked in the ______. Fill in the blank. I also wondered if we changed the Fourteenth Amendment. Does that exclude the Founding Fathers from being citizens? They were not born in the United States. I guess they are British colonialist.

The problem with any type of positive immigration law for our new immigrants is that the Dream Act and the changing of the Fourteenth Amendment are family reunification and anchor babies, respectively. I have heard the argument that the Dream Act will now have those new Permanent Residents, applying for others to come here. That is unlikely, because they do not have many ties in Mexico anyway. The anchor babies that are produced by the defective Fourth Amendment are ruining our country. Too many of them, especially around the border. If this is a country of laws that they argue, then follow the law. End of argument. Another thing that is funny is that minorities can relate to the bad unemployment situation we have now. That is how it always has been. Now that the majority population is experiencing it, it suddenly becomes a problem. We cannot not relate to that. Unemployment was normal I thought. Do not worry. We can make a stack of tortillas and pan of beans last all month. Another thing is depression. What is the deal about depression? I know losing a job, feeling ucky, being broke, and alienation makes people feel depressed, but all those aspects are normal for a lot of minorities. I was surprised that people actually get depressed about normal things. Even when I lost my law license. I was not the happiest camper, but I just lost my job. What is new? I grew up in the Projects where I used to fight the roaches to share the food. I was looking for a job when I found that one. Okay, enough of those self-evident truths. One last thing, for my mom. We kept our unit clean, but when you live somewhere where the units are stacked side by side and on top of each other, it only takes one family to mess everyone up!

As my clientele grew, the demands on my time grew too. I had to hire some lawyer(s) to help me with court. I told them what to expect. The government immigration lawyers know all the tricks and the government lawyers consist of the government lawyer and the Immigration Judge. I had previously mentioned that. I hired two lawyers at two separate times. I warned them that the government "lawyers" would gang up on you and make you agree to voluntary departure after the trial (which our clients would more than likely lose). I told them repeatedly, do not get intimidated by them. They are there to deport. I emphasized that we can appeal their decision and do not buckle under their pressure. It never worked. They would come back with their tails between their legs mumbling something about the judge while I was preparing their last check while telling them to go find another job. This was a moral, human rights and civil rights war and surrendering was not an option. I did not like it when other private immigration lawyers would act like friends to the government lawyers. I liked them as people, but thought they should get a different job instead of destroying families due to racist, hateful, immigration laws. I never talked to them around my clients, which meant I never talked to them because that was the only time I ever saw them. I just thought it was disrespectful to my clients to smooze with someone performing and enforcing unethical, godless laws that wanted to do them harm. I was practicing law for my clients, not competing for a popularity contest.

As mentioned, my practice was growing by leaps and bounds. The last few years before my suspension and eventual disbarment, the Judges would leave my cases for last for the Master Calendar Hearings (like the arraignments in criminal court), because I usually had around twenty cases while the other lawyers usually had one to three cases. I did not think much of it other than I had advertised and tried to do good work for my clients.

When I first started, I had trouble filling out the immigration forms. Yes, even with a J.D., the forms were confusing. The terms like petitioner, beneficiary, applicant, cosponsor, sponsor, start to blur into different meanings with different questions. I finally got it after a few years and my staff asking me what to do. You know, the best way to learn is to teach. If one did not specialize in immigration law, you were better off not doing it. Just like I could not do other areas of the law other than immigration, competently anyway. For example, the head of the public defenders came to do an immigration case and almost got his client deported. This was a guy that did murder cases routinely. I told him after the Master Calendar that if he needed help to call. He never did and I do not know what happened to his client either. I also became the "go to" immigration lawyer for legal advice to other lawyers and inspiring immigration lawyers. I would help anyone as much as I could. The last couple years I was practicing, the Police Department would refer clients to me when they got someone with immigration problems. Towards the end of my legal career, my life had become a series of deadlines and power naps. Something had to break.

CHAPER FOUR

The Beginning Of The End

When beginning to do immigration law, I had no idea what would happen. I just figured I would learn as much as I could, try to keep updated on the law, update my personal notes on the law and ask questions from more qualified practitioners. I had been going to Des Moines around 1998-99. Things were generally pretty slow, but I still went there regularly. At one of my last meetings in Des Moines, a lady from Lakely, Iowa, came down to Des Moines and told me she needed help in Lakely due to the huge immigrant population there. I believe there are a lot of chicken farms and other low paying jobs that attracted the immigrants. I had not heard from her in a while. Then all of a sudden, she came to my office in Ashtown and told me she was getting people work permits. I asked her how and she told me that it was from a form I gave her. I do not remember giving her any forms, but if I did, I probably gave her a variety of them because I carried a mobile office with me with all the necessary forms and my Steele's Book on Immigration, my favorite reference book. I still was not sure what form it was, but found out later it was the Asylum Application (I-589). You might have to refer back to when I wrote about INS/DHS asylum policy of issuing an EAD (Employment Authorization Document - Work Permit) if the application is not adjudicated by the agency in one hundred and fifty (150) days. You probably also remember how slow INS/DHS moves. One hundred and fifty days are nothing. When the new law was implemented around 1997, they did actually have a couple cases get adjudicated before one hundred and fifty days. So all the applications she was submitting were being granted EADs. Very good news, but what she was saying in the applications was the problem.

Martha was and I am sure still is a very good hearted and honest woman. Consequently, everything she wrote in the applications was brutally honest. As you will see, honesty can get you into trouble! She said they came here for a new life and to find a job! OMG! Did she think they were like normal previous immigrants!? I did not imagine the INS/DHS would like that and neither would the EOIR (Executive Office of Immigration Review - the IJs and the BIA Judges). The timeline at that time between applying and going to court was around a year. If I decided to take these cases, I would have to think of something or let those people get slaughtered. By the time I found out what she was doing, she had already filed a hundred or so. She was filing these for Mexicans and Mexicans generally do not qualify for asylum, despite the fact that I had previously won a Mexican asylum case.

Now I either had to think of something or run for the border myself, which reminds me, before I forget, I was ordered deported twice. Technical problem, typo, or on purpose? It was strangely funny getting those notices. Anyway, I knew that if someone files a frivolous asylum application, that there was a permanent bar to any other form of relief forever. So, I had better check to see what frivolous means, legally. Its plain dictionary meaning is like something worthless, waste of time or meritless. Maybe those honest answers on the application makes the application frivolous and those people are toast. Luckily, when I looked up what frivolous means, legally, in the EOIR Judge's Bench Handbook it said

> The BIA made a four-part test to see if a respondent has filed a frivolous application: (1) was there notice of consequences of filing a frivolous (2) the Immigration Judge must find that it was done knowingly; (3) has to be shown it was deliberately fabricated ; and (4) the immigrant must have a chance to explain any discrepancy. Matter of Y-L-, 24 I&N Dec. 151 (BIA 2007).

Very good. This definition is from the EOIR Judge's Bench Handbook with a four prong test to determine if an application could be deemed frivolous. Basically, as long as Martha was honest, frivolous should not be a problem. One had to "material fabricate a fact" in their case. Coming here for a job and a better life could not be more true. I also liked the fact that even if the application was considered frivolous, the applicant would still retain their due process rights to have the application heard based on Withholding of Deportation and CAT (Convention Against Torture), which if they are denied, they can be appealed as well. Remember,

I am trying to keep my clients here as long as I can, due to the immigration reform looming over the horizon, before the 2001disaster. No problem. If I can get these into court, my clients can practice their due process rights and at least have their day in court, appeal and keep their EAD (Employment Authorization Document), which they are entitled to have by law. Our ancestors are sure lucky they didn't have to buy one of these for the $100.00 filing fee! Anyway, before I go much further, I should explain due process. Everyone thinks of due process, like the Bill of Rights or Miranda Rights. Forget that. Your due process is whatever process is due, and nothing else. For example, divorce cases do not have juries. I should mention that the I-589 (asylum application) is also an application for Withholding of Removal (now) and CAT. Withholding of Removal is like asylum except the recipient of Withholding of Removal is not eligible for permanent residency and if I remember, they cannot get an EAD either. CAT relief was based on an international Torture Convention denouncing torture and using it as a form of relief against deportation/removal. The rules are narrower than asylum, but mundane and irrelevant, except for the fact that if asylum is denied, the applicant can still apply for those other forms of relief. I had a year to prepare a defense. The first thing I did was hire a paralegal with good research skills to develop a defense with periodic reviews with my paralegal for progress reports and so I could give him my input. I had him work full time just for this purpose. He was good. I was optimistic and nervous. Like I said, I had to go up against two lawyers with a propensity to deport. Martha kept filing them, but now I was going up to Lakey to explain the asylum process with them, the consequences of filing, like if you lose you go, the cost, and asked if they had any question. I only charged them the consultation fee of $40.00 and Martha filled out the applications. I do not know how much she was charging. That was between her and her clients. I did not retain any of these clients because there was no need to have them pay $75.00 a month while we wait for court. I told them after they are ordered to go to court, when the agency denied their application, to contact me if they wanted me to represent them. Consequently, I did not represent any of them other than a few that wanted me to take their case at that time anyway. I told everyone the same spill. The asylum process works the same for everyone, so there was no need to deviate my advice during consultations to anyone. It went like this. After you file the asylum application, you will receive a receipt with the day that it was received. That day starts there at one hundred and fifty days for their EAD. Consequently, they would have to file their EADs around the one hundredth and twentieth day to allow for the time for the Immigration Service in Lincoln to issue it. The timeframe on asylum cases was getting further and further backed up because of all the applications that were going to the Service Center in Lincoln, Nebraska, but generally the immigrants would receive a notice to go to an appointment with an asylum examiner approximately six months after the receipt was dated. If they won at the administrative level, that is primarily it. They would get a special asylee status and were eligible to adjust to a permanent resident in approximately a year. If not, the case would be submitted to the IJ for adjudication, de novo. That is supposed to mean that the judge is supposed to decide on the case, individually, regardless of the administrative record. This was one of those areas where the I.J. or the government attorney was not supposed to look at the administrative record for the new review of the application, which I am sure was not correctly followed. The judges routinely review the administrative record and have common place exparte communications. After all, they both have the same boss, the Department of Injustice. Oops. Anyway, after the asylum officer, who came here from Chicago for the interviews concluded the applicants were not eligible, they would refer the case to the IJ. The EOIR would coordinate with the district council (government lawyer) to set the Master Calendars. They would usually be about six months after the asylum interview. At the Master Calendar, as previously explained, I would tell the IJ what forms of relief my client would be attempting. For me as a deportation defense attorney (I kind of made up that name), my normal forms of relief were asylum (which includes withholding of removal and CAT), adjustment, or cancellation of removal. But before I did all that, I had to admit that my client was unlawfully present. In other words, I would have to admit their inadmissibility. It was something like an affirmative defense. For example, for one to claim the insanity defense (an affirmative defense) they first have to admit their client was guilty, then present their defense. Also, it was hard to admit that the person was not unlawfully present when his body was right in front of the Government IJ and government attorney. That was where that one experienced public defender almost got his client removed/deported. He did not admit that his client was inadmissible/unlawfully present; therefore, he did not have any forms of relief to present. This process was counterintuitive to criminal lawyers because they almost always plea not guilty at the arraignment, even if the victim's blood was all over the defendant while he was holding a smoking gun. On its face, that looks like the criminal lawyer was being dishonest about the plea and actually looks like the lawyer is wasting the time of the court with all the evidence. But, as a procedural tactic (although it looks dishonest) it makes the government prove their case and gives them time to prepare a defense. This is important later, because my procedural strategic tactics were later deemed abusive instead of tactical, by the person who ended my legal career. In hindsight, I should have gotten the permission of the IJ and the Bar before trying to practice law as I saw fit for my clients. Next, the IJ would give you a call-up date. That is a date that you have to have all your evidence to the EOIR in Chicago, with a copy to the government lawyer. In administrative law, we do not use the Federal Rules of Evidence. In other words, we do not have to offer our documents for the record. They are automatically entered and we did not have to defend any objections to the evidence because the objections are not applicable; consequently, the only thing that mattered was the *weight* of the evidence that the IJ gave them. The date the evidence is supposed to be submitted is called the call-up date, which was usually at least ten days before the Individual Hearing or the trial. By the time my license was suspended, the Individual Hearings were running around two years behind. I suspect it was partially due to all the increase in applications and the increase of the immigrant population. At the individual hearing if we win, permanent residency. If not, the IJ and government lawyers (the two prosecutors) would offer my client voluntary departure, in lieu of deportation. Voluntary departure (V.D.) allows the immigrant to leave without the stigma of deportation; therefore, they are not subject to the harsh consequences of deportation and they could eventually come back if there is a legal way to re-enter the U.S. Of course, I never accepted the decision and appealed. The avenues to enter the United States legally are so narrow in scope and restrictive, that accepting V.D. is just another avenue for a new hopeless hoop to jump. You may remember this is the pivotal point where you keep your client at all cost and do not accept voluntary departure, unless you wanted to get fired, as those attorneys whom I hired found out, despite the prosecutors' (IJ and government attorney) whining. The government attorney, would always say, "you're going to make bad law, if you appeal," while I was thinking they could not get much worse. Of course, the prosecutors were more worried about clearing their caseload than justice or due process. The appeal process could take from one to three years at the BIA level. Next, if the appeal fails, we could appeal to the Circuit Court, which in our district is the Eighth Circuit. The BIA appeal would stay (stop) the deportation, but with the Circuit Court, we would also have to file a "stay of deportation" along with the appeal to get a stay, which was rarely granted. Before 1996, the Circuit appeals were also mandatory stays, but that changed along with other restrictions on the ability for one to come here legal that was already very limited. For example, before the 1996 "reform" (more racist implementation of the law), we had a form of relief called the 212(C) relief where we could fight a person's blemished criminal record by showing the court that despite the record, the person is still eligible for relief in the form of permanent residency. For instance, if they had an assault on their record (even if it was a felony) we could point out that they only had this on their record, they are part of the PTA, they are in their church's choir, and they do extensive voluntary work, to tip the scales to overcome the criminal offense. That was taken away. Also, the government decided to change all felonies to aggravated felonies, including a lot of violations that are just misdemeanors. If one has a "aggravated felony" (including misdemeanors) they are not eligible for any relief, even if they are married to a U.S.C. A lot of difference from the Europeans emptying out their prisons to bring them here and the Elias Island procedure of twenty dollars, and I.D. and a short medical exam then immediate citizenship. Also, as already mentioned the further restrictions on Suspension of Deportation changing to Cancellation of Removal, the change from administratively adjusting a spouse of a U.S.C at the district office to Consular Processing, the changes in asylum law, and changes like making shoplifting (for example) an aggravated felony. The impact on misdemeanors changing to aggravated felonies excluded a lot of immigrants with petty crimes. Anyway, by time the Circuit Court appeal was finished the case may have lasted anywhere from four to six years, depending on the forms of relief. And if my client's time had ran out, I could admit a "motion to reopen" if any new facts were discovered or had changed to start the process over. That was the due process that was due. If the law is the law, then why weren't these same laws applicable to all people from all nations. Our ancestors were lucky to be born when they were born without all the restrictive laws now that would give them little or no chance to stay here.

I did want to touch on the practical aspects of immigration deportation defense when representing my clients at an asylum Individual Hearing. By the date of the Individual Hearing, all evidence should be in the EOIR in Chicago, but the IJ always asked if we wanted to submit more evidence at the trial or Individual Hearing. I did on occasion, but rarely. Next, the client would resign the application in the presence of the IJ, I guess as a testament to its veracity. Then I would start my questioning. My strategy, and I think the strategy of most lawyers in direct exam, is to emphasize our client's good points and touch upon any negative points that are potentially harmful before the government lawyer asked them questions concerning any negative aspects of the case. I had it down to a science, to the point when it was time for cross-examination, the government lawyer did not have any questions. I had my client already answer everything. I do not know if that bothered the government lawyer or not, as I was just trying to do my job. A lot of my asylum clients were victims of PTSD (Post Traumatic Stress Disorder) because they had been subject to beatings, rapes, kidnappings, watching their family get killed and/or beaten, threatened, and the list goes on. I believed my clients and often thought they were not telling me everything because it was too hurtful to have to relate and experience it again in their minds. They may have also had some memories blocked as our minds often use blackouts as a defense mechanism. Furthermore, most of my clients were just generally traumatized. Accordingly, they also had a demeanor of shyness, passiveness, and the inability to trust anyone. This would hurt in court because if someone testifies like they are hesitant, it appears to us anyway, like they may not be telling the truth. In Central American, the justice system is a lot different where being frightful is probably a good thing. Here timidity shows weakness, which affects one's credibility. Anyway, one of my main focuses when preparing my clients was to tell them to speak up and look the judge right in the eyes. I know that was hard for them to do, but I emphasized it, because it would often make the difference between a won or a lost case. The biggest factor in asylum cases is your client's demeanor. The IJ has little to go on but the subjective appearance of truthfulness. In other words, the immigrant's demeanor. Unfortunately, the documentation and evidence of asylum cases is few and far between. I mean what is the immigrant to do? Ask for a police report when it might be the police after him. Often if one family member is persecuted, the rest of the family is too. Consequently, it is even hard to get a letter from the other family members because they are afraid the persecutors will find out and hurt them. Medical reports would have been nice, but usually by time the person gets out of the hospital from their injuries, they are more interested in getting away than asking for their medical records to carry for hundreds of miles, for help. The main tools I had to use were their appearance of truthfulness and hoping the IJ was in a good mood, because it is the IJ's discretion that is pivotal in these cases. That is why I always told my client to cry if their story was traumatic and/or sad. This was especially important when my female clients had been subject to beatings and rapes. I have a lot of stories I could tell, but it brings back too many painful memories. I do not know how many times I had to stop with my questions and give my clients a Kleenex. As stated, we asylum practitioners are at a big disadvantage because of the lack of evidence. The government attorney would routinely damage my client's testimony and credibility because of the lack of evidence. For example, when I had my client show the IJ gunshot wounds or scars from beatings, he would say that probably happened when they were gang banging in Los Angeles. That would upset me, especially when the IJ appeared to agree and there was no evidence to support such a prejudicial assertion. That happened more times than I care to remember.

There were some bright moments though. An IJ came here as a visiting IJ from Texas and he wanted me and the Lead Counsel for the government to go into his office (chambers) and discuss the case. The first thing he said was that he was going to grant my client asylum. You should have seen government's attorney's jaw drop and he almost dropped the papers he was holding. I was walking on a cloud that day. Another incident occurred when a new client came into my office the day before her asylum case and wanted me to represent her. I usually charged $75.00 a month, but charged her two hundred dollars ($200.00) because I had one night to prepare for her trial. She got her permanent residency the next day. Good for her. Now tell me, when have you ever seen a lawyer do anything for $200.00? We know we've got licenses to steal, not because we may be good or not. It is just that the system is set up as a monopoly. Basically, law school prepares one to pass the bar exam. I know of some students who only went to class to take the final then passed the bar exam, anyway. Consequently, Blow

Joe off the streets can read and pass the test. Ally BaBa, you got a lawyer. Anyway, one last memorable experience I had was on a criminal case where this lady claimed her boyfriend dragged her across a parking lot for about thirty feet. She weighed about 300 pounds. He weighed maybe 120 pounds. I asked her on the witness stand how much she weighed. The courtroom got quiet. She looked at me indignantly, and the judge dismissed her complaint.

Okay, that was part of some of the procedural and practical aspects to keep in mind. My problem was convincing or persuading the court to look at all my arguments, getting testimony and any further documents in evidence, and making a sufficient record for the potential appeals for these Mexican Asylum cases. I had a lot of bites in the apple, so to speak, to do this. First off, with the call-up date a year or so ahead, then at the Individual Hearing, the IJ would also take any additional evidence despite the call-up. So in my mind, with these difficult cases coming, I had a least two years to prepare for court. I had the application, my paralegal's report in support of social group asylum for the immigrants and the benefit of submitting any evidence at the call-up and the day of the hearing, and if lost, I should still have a decent appeal if I made a good record. That was my plan and the due process we afford our new immigrants. Was this a dilatory practice? Meaning, was I doing this to just keep the case going and keep my clients here? Yes. In my mind, anyway, my clients were paying me to keep them here or literally, "buying time." As mentioned, this was important if the law changed. If they are not here, they would not be eligible for any new laws; and furthermore, they were paying for their time here at $75.00 a month for any matter that would occur in their case. In the back of mind, I knew I was following Code of Professional Responsibility because, as a lawyer, we are supposed to be zealous in representation. It read like this:

> DR 7-102(A) In his representation of a client, a lawyer shall not:
>
> (2) **Knowingly advance a claim or defense that is unwarranted under existing law, except that he may advance such claim or defense if it can be supported by good faith argument for an extension, modification, or reversal of existing law. . . .**

Of course, my strategy was to use the Code of Professional Responsibilities language, ". . .**except that he may advance such claim or defense if it can be supported by good faith argument for an extension, modification, or reversal of existing law.**" That is why I hired the paralegal, full time, in combination of my knowledge of asylum law (which was really my specialty, within the specialty of being a deportation defense attorney) to clear the hurdle by bringing forth, "by good faith" argument. I guess I forgot to look at the invisible footnote stating, "except for Undesirables." Before I get too much further, it is important to look at the nuances of asylum.

When anyone thinks of asylum they thing of political asylum. You know, we will take refugees from war torn nations for humanitarian purposes. Historically, as previously noted, this country was a beacon for any suppressed populations, especially the economically depressed like the Irish during the Irish Potato Famine and other circumstances forcing most Europeans and others to arrive here for jobs, higher wages and opportunity and to escape economic conditions. Sound familiar? I referred to an article called Immigration to the United States, prepared by Economic History Services, authored by, Raymond L. Cohn, which states the primary reasons for migration to the United States are as follows:

The Causes of Immigration

Economic historians generally believe no single factor led to immigration. In fact, different studies have tried to explain immigration by emphasizing different factors, with the first important study being done by Thomas (1954). The most recent attempt to comprehensively explain immigration has been by Hatton and Williamson (1998), who focus on the period between 1860 and 1914. Hatton and Williamson view immigration from a country during this time as being caused by up to five different factors: (a) the difference in real wages between the country and the United States; (b) the rate of population growth in the country 20 or 30 years before; (c) the degree of industrialization and urbanization in the home country; (d) the volume of previous immigrants from that country or region; and (e) economic and political conditions in the United States. To this list can be added factors not relevant during the 1860 to 1914 period, such as the potato famine, the movement from sail to steam, and the presence or absence of immigration restrictions.

The only time employer sanction started in our history (with Reagan's amnesty) is when immigrants decided to come to work for next to nothing, and not even having a say in it. Not because they want low wages and asked for them, but because the "Job Makers" can now have another class of people to take advantage of, similar to slavery, who are forced to take what is given to them. They are the ones who lower the wages not the immigrants. But because the "Job Makers" actually take down the wages by paying our old, yet, new immigrants less. It is also surprising the immigrants are coming for the same reasons as everyone else, with the exception of the intentional genocide of the Native Americans. That is why when I hear the argument that they (the new immigrants) should come just like their ancestors did, legally, I try not to throw up. Sorry, walking off a boat with twenty dollars and an I.D. is not all that is needed now. I guess I was way out of line that I thought our new immigrants should be afforded the same standards as our previous "legally present" immigrants. I know we can argue that their ancestors were subject to discriminations too. Discriminations are one thing, exclusions, deportations, and employer sanctions, which our new immigrants have to suffer, is a distinct inseparable, indefensible argument to defend, and circumstances their ancestors did not have to endure. In a heated argument with one of my conservative buddies, he flatly told me, that Mexicans are a conquered people, I guess from the Mexican-American War, so that was the end of my argument. I had nothing to say. I did appreciate his honesty and is still one of my best friends. I always figure we are where we are because of our history. Consequently, I will look briefly at the Mexican-American War and the Treaty of Hildalgo. David Saville Muzzey's popular 1911 text "American History" explained the Mexican War to school children of the early twentieth century, told why the United States seized California in 1846, and how the U.S. ended the Texas-Mexico border dispute. The Treaty of Guadalupe-Hidalgo, which officially ended the war, was signed in 1848, just nine days after gold was discovered at Sutter's Mill in California. Dr. Muzzey's text also gave great insight into contemporary American thinking about "Manifest Destiny." This text, and its revised editions, was still in classroom use as late as the 1940's.

The Mexican War
by David Saville Muzzey, Ph.D.
Barnard College, Columbia University, New York

Mexico refuses to recognize the
Annexation of Texas.

> The annexation of Texas was a perfectly fair transaction. For nine years, since the victory of San Jacinto in 1836, Texas had been an independent republic, whose reconquest Mexico had not the slightest chance of effecting. In fact, at the very moment of annexation, the Mexican government, at the suggestion of England, had agreed to recognize the independence of Texas, on condition that the republic should not join itself to the United States. We were not taking Mexican territory, then, in annexing Texas. The new state had come into the Union claiming the Rio Grande as her southern and western boundary. By the terms of annexation all boundary disputes with Mexico were referred by Texas to the government of the United States. President Polk sent John Slidell of

Louisiana to Mexico in the autumn of 1845 to adjust any differences over the Texan claims. But though Slidell labored for months to get a hearing, two successive presidents of revolution-torn Mexico refused to recognize him, and he was dismissed from the country in August, 1846.

Taylor attacked on the Rio Grande.

The massing of Mexican troops on the southern bank of the Rio Grande, coupled with the refusal of the Mexican government to receive Slidell, led President Polk to order General Zachary Taylor to move to the borders. Taylor marched to the Rio Grande and fortified a position on the northern bank. The Mexican and the American troops were thus facing each other across the river. When Taylor refused to retreat to the Nueces, the Mexican commander crossed the Rio Grande, ambushed a scouting force of 63 Americans, and killed or wounded 16 of them (April 24, 1846).

The United States accepts War with Mexico.

When the news of the attack reached Washington early in May, Polk sent a special message to Congress, concluding with these words:

"We have tried every effort at reconciliation... But now, after reiterated menaces, Mexico has passed the boundary of the United States [the Rio Grande], has invaded our territory and shed

American blood upon the American soil. She has proclaimed that hostilities have commenced, and that the two nations are at war. As war exists, and, notwithstanding all our efforts to avoid it, exists by the act of Mexico herself, we are called upon by every consideration of duty and patriotism to vindicate with decision the honor, the rights, and the interests of our country."

The House and Senate, by very large majorities (174 to 14, and 40 to 2), voted 50,000 men and $10,000,000 for the prosecution of the war.

Taylor invades Mexico.

Meanwhile, General Taylor had driven the Mexicans back to the south bank of the Rio Grande in the battles of Palo Alto and Resaca de la Palma. Six days after the vote of Congress sanctioning the war, he crossed the Rio Grande and occupied the Mexican frontier town of Matamoros, whence he proceeded during the summer and autumn of 1846 to capture the capitals of three of the Mexican provinces.

The Occupation of California and New Mexico.

As soon as hostilities began, Commodore Sloat, in command of our squadron in the Pacific, was ordered to seize California, and General [Stephen Watts] Kearny was sent to invade New Mexico. The occupation of California was practically undisputed. Mexico had only the faintest shadow of authority in the province, and the 6000 white inhabitants made no objection to seeing the flag of the United States raised over their forts. Kearny started with 1800 men from Fort Leavenworth, Kansas, in June, and on the eighteenth of August defeated the force of 4000 Mexicans and Indians which disputed his occupation of Santa Fé. After garrisoning this important post he detached Colonel Doliphan with 850 men to march through the northern provinces of Mexico and effect a juncture with General Taylor at Monterey, while he himself with only 100 men continued his long journey of 1500 miles to San Diego, California, where he joined Sloat's successor, Stockton." I'd.

Taylor's Victory at Buena Vista.

After these decided victories and uninterrupted marches of Taylor, Kearny, Sloat, Stockton, and Doniphan, the Mexican government was offered a fair chance to treat for peace, which it refused. Then President Polk decided, with the unanimous consent of his cabinet, to strike at the heart of Mexico. General Winfield Scott, a hero of the War of 1812, was put in command of an army of about 12,000 men, to land at Vera Cruz and fight his way up the mountains to the capital city of Mexico. Santa Anna, who, by the rapid shift of revolutions, was again dictator in Mexico, heard of this plan to attack the capital and hastened north with 20,000 troops to surprise and destroy Taylor's army before Scott should have time to take Vera Cruz. But Taylor, with an army one-fourth the size of Santa Anna's, drove the Mexicans back in the hotly contested battle of Buena Vista (February 23, 1847), securing the Californian and New Mexican conquests. Santa Anna hastened southward to the defense of the city of Mexico.

Scott take the city of Mexico.

Scott took Vera Cruz in March and worked his way slowly but surely, against forces always superior to his own, up to the very gates of Mexico (August, 1847). Here he paused, by the President's orders, to allow the Mexicans another chance to accept the terms of peace which the United States offered,-the cession by Mexico of New Mexico and California in return for a large payment of money. The Mexican commissioners, however, insisted on having both banks of the Rio Grande and all of California up to the neighborhood of San Francisco, besides receiving damages for injuries inflicted by the American troops in their invasions. These claims were preposterous, coming from a conquered country, and there was nothing left for Scott to do but to resume military operations. Santa Anna defended the capital with a force of 30,000 men, but the Mexicans were no match for the American soldiers. Scott stormed the fortified hill of Chapultepec and advanced to the gates of the city. On the thirteenth of September his troops entered the Mexican capital and raised the Stars and Strips over "the palace of the Montezumas."

Polk's Efforts to secure Peace.

From the beginning of the war Polk had been negotiating for peace. He had kept Slidell in Mexico long after the opening of hostilities and had sent Nicholas Trist as special peace commissioner to join Scott's army at Vera Cruz and to offer Mexico terms of peace at the earliest possible moment. He had allowed Santa Anna to return to Mexico from his exile in Cuba in the summer of 1846, because the wily and treacherous dictator held out false promises of effecting a reconciliation between Mexico and the United States. He had asked Congress for an appropriation of $2,000,000 for peace negotiations when General Taylor was still near the Rio Grande, ten days before General Kearny had taken Santa Fé and the province of New Mexico, and before General Scott's campaign had been thought of.

The Treaty of Guadalupe-Hidalgo.

When the Mexican commissioners made advances for peace at the beginning of the year 1848, they were given terms almost as liberal as those offered them before Scott had stormed and occupied their capital. By the treaty concluded at Guadalupe-Hidalgo, February 2, 1848, Mexico was required to cede California and New Mexico to the United States and to recognize the Rio Grande as the southern and western boundary of Texas. In return, the United States paid Mexico $15,000,000 cash and assumed some $3,250,000 more in claims of American citizens on the Mexican government. Considering the facts that California was scarcely under Mexican control at all and might have been taken at any moment by Great Britain, France, or Russia; that New Mexico was still the almost undisturbed home of Indian tribes; that the land from the Nueces to the Rio Grande was almost a desert; and that the American troops were in possession of the Mexican capital, the terms offered Mexico were very generous. Polk was urged by many to annex the whole country of Mexico to the United States, but he refused to consider such a proposal." I'd.

The Justice of the Mexican War.

The Mexican War has generally been condemned by American historians as "the foulest blot on our national honor," a war forced upon Mexico by slaveholders greedy for new territory, a perfect illustration of La Fontaine's fable of the wolf picking a quarrel with the lamb solely for an excuse to devour him. But Mexico had insulted our flag, plundered our commerce, imprisoned our citizens, lied to our representatives, and spurned our envoys. As early as 1837 President Jackson said that Mexico's offenses "would justify in the eyes of all nations immediate war." To be sure we were a strong nation and Mexico a weak one. But weakness should not give immunity to continued and open insolence. We had a right to annex Texas after that republic had maintained its independence for nine years; yet Mexico made annexation a cause of war. We were willing to discuss the boundaries of Texas with Mexico; but our accredited envoy was rejected by two successive Mexican presidents, who were afraid to oppose the war spirit of their country. We even refrained from taking Texas into the Union until Great Britain had interfered so far as to persuade Mexico to recognize the independence of Texas if she would refuse to join the United States.

The Moral Aspect of the Annexation of Texas.

If there was anything disgraceful in the expansionist program of the decade 1840-1850, it was not the Mexican War, but the annexation of Texas. The position of the abolitionists on this question was clear and logical. They condemned the annexation of Texas as a wicked extension of the slavery area, notwithstanding all arguments about "fulfilling our manifest destiny" or "attaining our natural boundaries." To annex Texas might be legally right, they said, but it was morally wrong. James Russell Lowell, in his magnificent poem "The Present Crisis" (1844), warned the annexationists that "They enslave their children's children who make compromise with sin." We certainly assumed a great moral responsibility when we annexed

Texas. However, it was not to Mexico that we were answerable, but to the enlightened conscience of the nation.

Completion of the Program of Expansion.

With our acquisition of the Oregon territory to the forty-ninth parallel by the treaty of 1846 with Great Britain, and the cession of California and New Mexico by the treaty of Guadalupe-Hidalgo in 1848, the boundaries of the United States reached practically their present limits. The work of westward extension was done. Expansion, the watchword of the decade 1840-1850, was dropped from our vocabulary for fifty years, and the immense energies of the nation were directed toward finding a plan on which the new territory could be organized in harmony with the conflicting interests of the free and slave sections of our country.

IN: An American History, by David Saville Muzzey. Boston : Ginn Company, 1911

I could comment further, but this country was and still appears to be a course of the rationalization of immoral expansionism. Iraq, and Afganistan, for example. I could also talk about the way the Treaty was not enforced especially when the land was taken from the Mexicans already living there after they were promised to be able to keep their land. Maybe, some of you are aware that most the treaties were not honored, you know like with the

> Native Americans. Why should it be any different for the Mexicans? It wasn't. I also find it comical when people talk about all the Mexicans taking over the United States. Oh, I forgot, a third of the U.S. use to be Mexico. That may be a good reason for some Mexican looking people hanging around.
>
> Although, it looks like we have shifted to another system of immigration since our brothers and sisters from Europe came here, I am honestly glad that our former immigrants were not subject to trivial conditions imposed to limit their presence here, like the new immigrants. It just seems so harsh when you think about how their settlements were established.

Anyway, it looked like I had my ducks in order and at least a couple of years to prepare a rational defense and all my due process rights established. I knew the day would come when I had to present one of these cases to the IJ or it would be the end for Martha and now some of my clients. In law and probably like other areas of any job, sometimes we have to do "damage control." You know, if things don't look real promising, you do what you can to minimize your damages. There was talk about the applications that Martha was submitting as being bad in some way. Legally, I could not see how. But rumors, ignorance, and the deportation disposition of the INS/DHS did not help. I was approached by the lead immigration government attorney one day when he implicated me in filling out one of the applications Martha was doing. He made some type of comment that I had Martha do the applications so I can be twice removed from them. I just looked at him and answered what I thought was his sarcastic remark with another one. Yes. There were also rumors going around that Mexicans are not eligible for asylum, which I knew was wrong since I won a Mexican asylum case previously. There were also rumors that economic asylum was not longer available like it was for our European brothers, for example, the Potato Famine in Ireland. I had looked at case law which explained economic asylum is available as long as there was a nexus with one of the legal enumerated areas of asylum law. I had at least a couple of years to make that nexus along with new case law that appeared to be developing concerning economic asylum. There were also rumors of me doing these cases for money. As previously stated, I had Martha fill out the forms and if her clients wanted to hire me they could, but I did not want to do anything until they get their court date so I could enter my appearance then and not waste their money while the application was pending. If I said I made two or three thousand dollars off all the cases, in the final analysis, I would have been exaggerating. My office was already generating close to two hundred thousand dollars a year of income for me. I did not need these cases, but I could not watch these people get slaughtered by INS/DHS either. So I took on the enormous task of damage control.

Usually, at Master Calendars all that is required is to state your causes of action and the merits of your case are examined at the Individual Hearing or the trial. But Judge Queries was deviating that normal procedural operation when the issue of Mexican Asylum cases came before him. He had now determined that the merits of this case without testimony, evidence, or any other due process consideration. I had a general respect for the IJ because they are in a position of authority and civility and the recognition of that authority was important. The IJs also knew I was going to stick up for my clients like I thought I was supposed to. You know our system is based on an adversarial form of justice. Each side argues for their position and the judge makes a determination. There was something wrong going on that day. I could see it in the prosecutors eyes and could cut the nervousness in the air with a knife. Judge Queriers, a Mexican American (who in my opinion forgot where he came from, like most anti-immigration people) started drilling me on the substantive immigration laws and the argument I was trying to put forth. I explained to him what I was doing and answered all his questions that he appeared to be attempting to trip me up on. That was funny. Immigration is about all I felt I knew anything about. Our discussion was not reaping any progress and was starting to get heated and ugly. I knew what my job was and I knew what his job was as a prosecutor, I mean judge. You see, the government attorney should have been arguing the case, not the judge. But since they are one and the same, I guess it did make sense. To make a long story short, he deemed the application frivolous, not because it contained material misrepresentations of any facts, but because he thought I should not do them or something. It had to be something because he had no problem in deviating from local procedural protocol and denying my client's due process right to trial or any of the due process that was legally due, as previously discussed. What he did is like my famous murderer analogy points out. The murderer goes to his arraignment (the Master Calendar) to state he is not guilty even though the victim's blood is all over him and he is caught with the smoking gun. But this time the judge thinks his case is not good, so forget the murderer's rights, like his trial and deems him guilty without the benefit of evidence, testimony, or argument. Well, what does work for murderers in a criminal case, I guess does not apply to those damn illegal immigrants who managed to cross a line on the ground or river. That was the major problem, Queriers, had set a precedence for all the other Mexican asylum cases, despite the fact that they really exist and are legal. Especially, because I learned what frivolous meant from the Judge's Handbook which he obviously forgot or never read it. Or it may have been orders from his boss, the Department of Injustice. Darn I should have gone into corporate or tax law so I could find corporations loopholes and hopefully some day lobby for them!

That was around the end. Of course, I appealed his obvious erroneous decision and found out later that his decision was overturned by the BIA when I was indicted for mail fraud and money laundering, but I'll get to that. Now other lawyers, who obviously had not done their homework, were jumping on the bandwagon. I was getting beaten down by a prosecutor judge and now the rest of the ignorant immigration lawyers. Now that the word was out that I had filed "frivolous" Mexican Asylum cases, I started getting complaints by concerned clients, especially in the northern, Iowa area, by an ignorant new immigration lawyer named Joe Bone, who agreed with Judge "I don't know the law.". I was responding to the complaints by the Bar telling them I knew what I was doing and everything will be okay once I have a chance to present my case. They were not convinced, so I had my license suspended.

Well, I told you a lot about the procedural aspects of Asylum law, now I have to discuss the substantive areas of asylum law, as painlessly as possible. Asylum is basically when people from other countries who need help due to political, religious, race, nationality, or a particular social group, persecution. Persecution is where one is persecuted (harmed) by a group of people that the government cannot control or it can be the government itself that is doing the persecution. Now, persecution can be past or present persecution. Present persecution is easily defined, but past persecution has to be so severe that a reasonable person would still be fearful to return to there home country. Refugees are those who are persecuted in there home country where the U. S. Consulate/Embassy grants those persecuted entry on any of those grounds listed, if it's a reasonable subjective fear of persecution. Asylees are people who are granted asylum by the U.S. while in the U.S. Similar to those children coming to the border, as many of our ancestors did. Of course, when they reach the border they have to convince the Border Patrol that they have a reviewable claim then they are processed as previously discussed. This was important with my economic persecution theory involving the Mexican's government unwillingness and/or the inability to promote good and fair economic policies for their population. Also, asylum is not just based on political, race, nationality, religious grounds, it is also based on a social group category, which encompasses every other circumstance, including but not limited to gay rights, domestic abuse and economic asylum. Economic asylum or resettlement by our historical immigrants was always acceptable. Why had it changed for Mexicans and other Central Americans?

My focus on the cases had to deal with the nexus between the five grounds for asylum, race, religion, nationality, political and social group (which are people being economically persecuted). For some reason, (discrimination), unlike the Irish who were saved from the Potato Famine who came here to escape starvation like children and others are suffering in Central America, now these new staving victims subjected to economic persecution by a government that adopts policies to impoverish an already impoverished nation, now has to have a nexus between not being able to make a living or eat, with any of the five grounds of asylums, except social group, because they are the social group, in this case, a group of economically suppressed people due to the government's prosecutorial economic policies. If this was the case our current Irish population would be decimated. Oh I forgot, we are a country of laws and they came here legally. Can anyone see what's wrong with this picture? I know there is fairness and there is the law, like slavery, Jim Crow, and women shouldn't vote. I was also going to tie in the danger of the Cartels and the common occurrence that once INS/DHS leave them at the border the are subject to assaults and robberies. After all, they just left the U.S., they must have money.

Laws are based on the riches' whim who are the law makers with little notice to those with marginal existence with few exceptions.

For example, one new development was NAFTA which actually caused northen immigration due to its negative consequences. Here is some analysis of the impact of NAFTA.

The impact of NAFTA on wages and incomes in Mexico by Carlos Salas, La Red de Investigadores y Sindicalistas Para Estudios Laborales.

The decline in real wages and the lack of access to stable, well-paid jobs are critical problems confronting Mexico's workforce. While NAFTA has benefited a few sectors of the economy, mostly maquiladora industries and the very wealthy, it has also increased inequality and reduced incomes and job quality for the vast majority of workers in Mexico.

The burden of proof an applicant must show is that she has a well-founded fear of persecution in her home country on account of either race, religion, nationality, political opinion, or membership in a particular social group. The applicant can demonstrate her well-founded fear by demonstrating that she has a subjective fear (or apprehension) of future persecution in her home country that is objectively reasonable. There are actually volumes of books explaining asylum and all its tentacles but that definition will suffice. For example, I do not see the language that states that the fear of prosecution is a fear that the controlling government is not willing or able to control persecutors and it can be the government itself doing the persecution.

There had been case law addressing economic asylum. I was hanging my hat on a 1994 case that was still good on the issue of combining one of the five group categories with economic persecution which reads in part and forgive me, but here it is,

Osorio v. I.N.S., 18 F.3d 1017, 62 USLW 2565 (2nd Cir. Mar 07, 1994). This was a case where a immigrant was denied asylum due to the fact that economic refugees are no longer allowed in the United States like it was for their European counterparts, who basically came here for that reason. One argument is that there is not enough room for everybody. One, not everyone wants to come here. Two, it is not how many people are here that is the problem, it is who the people are. Otherwise, we would have population control measures, similar to China. Anyway, our new immigrant Mr. Osorio was initially denied because they said he came here as an economic refugee, whom are bad, legally. But the court determined that due to his union affiliation which caused his economic plight, that that created a nexus so he was granted asylum.

Good, a Federal District Court was on my side, but there is more. Sorry, but this is necessary. The following is some of the pertinent portions of the case that gave my new calling hope and assurance that under current immigration law, economic asylum does still exist under certain circumstances (finding an nexus) between economic deprivation/persecution and one of the four remaining grounds, because I would consider the social group with no control over their livelihood due to persecutional government economic policies (political persecution), viable. I intended to use the implementation of NAFTA, the Cartels, and the violence in Mexico as grounds for asylum. I knew at least, under current law, due process, and civil procedure that at least my clients would at least have their day in court. As you will see, most the stuff I learned in law school and practicing immigration law the last twelve years, was rubbish. If possible, read the entire case. Just google the name or case citation.

. . . As the U.N. Handbook observed:

> The distinction between an economic migrant and a refugee is ... sometimes blurred in the same way as the distinction between economic and political measures in an applicant's country of origin is not always clear. Behind economic measures affecting a person's livelihood, there may be racial, religious or political aims or intentions directed against a particular group. U.N. Handbook, at §§ 62-64.

Wasn't that great?! Okay, maybe. At worst, I had something to hang my hat on and develop while I have the next two years to prepare, build my theories and present a rational argument for my clients. While up to now, I had followed the law, procedurally and substantially, did my homework, had thirteen years of experience behind me, had my ducks in order and was ready to go except for one problem. My license had been suspended.

Where was my due process? Well, I did get what process was due. A lawyer can get his license immediately suspended if he is considered a danger to society and a menace to the administration of justice. I guess that was me, but I knew once I got my disciplinary hearing, I would explain everything and everything would be fine. How could I expect everyone or anyone to know all the intricacies of immigration asylum law? Even Judge Queriers did not know the legal definition of frivolous and how it relates to asylum applications.

One might logically conclude that one should have his opinion heard before they lose their license, but we have to protect the public of unscrupulous attorneys. But it did make sense, I was potentially hurting the majority public by legally allowing Mexicans to stay in their communities, state and cities. I was an unaware, impetuous, catalyst to the unending saga supporting the "invasion." While all I was doing was trying to follow the language of the law in an effort to zealously represent my client. My main problem was that I was over optimistic, motivated, and ambitious. The terms unscrupulous, dishonest, incompetent, and plain bad were names I invariably adopted. I had a bad feeling when this happened that the other few immigration deportation defense attorneys would not do anything either from the simple facts that they were ignorant of the pertinent law or just plain scared to offend the powers of those in authority, who recognize the plain letter law of the land should change when their agenda is not being met. Unfortunately, I was right. None of my former friends and colleagues supported me in any fashion. Rather, they all had some disparaging comment about what I did. I could say more about them, but they are all supposed to be smart people who know the law. Okay.

Well, it did not end there. I think because Judge Queriers deemed by submission of the above noted Mexican Asylum case frivolous, everyone was jumping on the bandwagon. Not only the ignorant attorney Bone, (a local inexperienced attorney who took the opportunity to use my misfortune as a way to get my clients and publicity, by writing complaints for my clients saying they did not know what they did), but also the clerks at the INS District Office. Now whenever my clients went in there, the clerks would tell my clients I am messing up their case, stealing their money, and that asylum is not for Mexicans. Everyone had turned to police, judge, jury and executioner. I had immediately appealed the case, which means that Queries order was not a final order. Once a decision is appealed, there is a stay on the decision, negating the IJ's order until a final order (ruling) is set forth by the BIA. Now the Bar was also convinced that I had somehow deceived my clients or at least filed frivolous applications that preemptively deprived them from any type of immigration relief. Near the end of 2002, Tom Stone, one of the disciplinary attorneys came to my office with a stack full of complaints, primarily sent by Bone saying that I was not doing the cases correctly and he also stated that my clients were not aware that they were filing asylum cases. As I said, I do not know Spanish, but I do not have any reason to believe my interpreters would not tell the clients everything I said accurately. A lot of clients were concerned, but I assured them everything is okay. I tried to call Bone a few times, but he never responded. I was just going to assure him everything is fine. I did not want to go through the explanation of my legal theories and my strategical tactics, which I had learned over the years but I probably should have, being that he was an inexperienced immigration lawyer. I had only seen him once or twice in immigration court and was not very impressed with his knowledge or skills. Nonetheless, I suppose because he had a J.D. he was now the immigration authority. After my suspension, Bone had an interview with a reporter from the local newspaper and was explaining that I could do some COR (Cancellation of Removal) by getting the cases in court, but that they are very difficult and the law limits them to four thousand a year and any additional cases would not be eligible. If he knew anything, he would have known I had won at least half my COR (and the old Suspension cases) cases and that even if the limit is met in a year, it rolls over to the next year, according to immigration law. It is that kind of subtle differences that can make or break a case, that he obviously ignorantly could not explain accurately. Plus, he was scaring my clients into firing me and hiring him, for a three thousand dollar ($3,000.00) retainer, while I was charging them a couple hundred to start then $75.00 a month. Where's the justice? Furthermore, it is an ethical violation to take a case without firing the first attorney. It was explained in law school like this. We are not doctors. We can not ethically give second opinions. I guess the disciplinary committee forgot about that obvious violation by Mr. Bone. I had some of my former clients wanting me to complain about him, because once they found out he was not any good and did not want to give a refund, they did not want him. I did not have the inclination or time to be writing complaints about other lawyers' work. So I never did.

Now I was starting to understand why all my Latino law student classmates, left the Midwest as soon as they got their degree.

My intention in this section was to talk a little about when I got my license suspended around January or February of 2003. As previously explained, my life had became a series of deadlines and power naps. Every week, I would tell myself if I can make it through this week, I can make it through anything. I was one of those people who intentionally took on more than I knew I could do. I just figured even if I do not finish everything I set out to do, by piling more obligations and responsibilities on myself, I would get more things done then I would otherwise, by not piling tons of work on myself and my staff. I also was rationalizing that by telling myself that God would not give me more than I could handle. Then at the end of every week, I would tell myself, now that I made it through another week, I can do anything. But the work and stress was taking a toll on me physically that I did not see at the time. I had gotten a back surgery around 1997, and had reinjured by back again around 1999 and my doctor told me I probably needed another surgery, but I could not do it because of my clients. So I just took pain killers (which I hate because they made me sleepy), and got those steroid blocks that helped temporarily. Plus, I had developed high blood pressure around 2002. It corresponded with the time Tom Stone, from the disciplinary committee, came to show me all those complaints. That same day he came, I ended up in the Emergency Room because I had a headache I could not shake. When I got there my pressure was like 250/200. I never really associated stress with physical health, but now I think they are pretty closely related. I also decided to get my back surgery in December of 2002, because that is generally when court slows down; when the Immigration Judges and government attorneys celebrate the Federal Holidays. I had taken the pain long enough and one knows when it is time. I had been afraid to get my back surgery because I knew it would interfere with my case load and clients, as I had previously mentioned.

CHAPTER FIVE

Nearly The End

As previously mentioned, my license was suspended late 2003. I had previously been visited by Tom Stone from Nebraska disciplinary office. He had about 10 complaints about the asylum applications and I believe all of them were from Bone. His allegations were that people didn't know what they were signing and that Mexicans are ineligible for asylum. I had previously won a Mexican asylum case so I just figured he was inexperienced and ignorant of law. Immigration law can get pretty complicated and I know he was a new guy on the block so I kind of blew it off because he didn't know what he was talking about. Nonetheless, I made a pretty lengthy response to the allegations because substantively and procedurally everything would eventually work out. I assured Mr. Stone of that, but evidently my response wasn't convincing or they believed that other lawyer that only been an immigration lawyer for maybe a year, knew more than me. Consequently, my license was suspended. When a lawyer gets his license suspended, I learned, he has to contact his clients, give them back their file and send them a letter to get another lawyer. I had 500 active cases so my staff was busy getting all the letters together and answering all the phone calls from all the news about my license being suspended. I had back surgery a couple months before this so I wasn't doing too well physically. The easiest way to explain this is, the shit hit the fan! It took nearly a year before my disciplinary hearing. Just enough time to use all my savings, lose all my employees. and eventually not being able to pay the rent and they locked the door to my office and changed the locks. My health was getting worse and I stopped going to my office. Everything from my law practice was in there, except what ever people had taken, which I had no idea of. In the meantime I was trying to recover from my back surgery and trying to figure out how to maintain my $20,000 a month fixed expenses. I think I literally saw on the wall in my bedroom, which is bigger than the apartment I live in now, you're going to lose everything. This is also the time my precious ex-wife kept threatening me with divorce if didn't pay her bills and stop paying mine. I other words, the marriage vows for better or worse, were meaningless. We had a another five bedroom house that was pretty nice, so she just told me pay her bills, we'll keep the money she said she had and when I run out of money we'll move to the other house. I eventually got the largest divorce file in Nebraska history, but that's another book. Things were looking pretty bad, but on the other hand losing a law license really didn't seem to be too big of a problem. Maybe my livelihood would be taken away, but I was looking for job when I found that one. I grew up part of my childhood in the projects so whatever happens, is cool. Besides that, I knew once I explained the law at my disciplinary hearing, then they would understand because what I was doing was the law and statutory. But the Bar Association was doing everything they could to get my license anyway. They asked me to give them my license to make it easier on them, but I didn't do nothing wrong, I didn't think. So I told them no.

I found out that my referee (judge) at the disciplinary hearing was going to be, a lawyer who worked in a Law Clinic. He occasionally took students to immigration court for the Clinic, so I thought he may be knowledgeable enough to handle the case, but in hindsight he already had his mind made up and was ignorant on handling immigration law and legal Immigration doctrine to real life. By time my court date ensued, around ten months later, I was broke and my marriage was less than a joke, but I was hopeful. One thing came good out of it though. I was unemployed, so I had all those months to stay with my son and daughter. I was hopeful because I had a winning case, even though the Bar Association put more charges against me, relating to the same subject matter. They said I was still filing asylum claims which is true. Anyone can fill out forms, as I previously explained, but I guess in my case, no. I also took passport pictures I thought anyone can do, but they told me no pictures, either. I was also trying to collect money people owed me, but in my case, no. Lawyers are entitled to their fees before the suspension or disbarment, but they made an exception for me not to receive the money I had earned. I didn't respond to the Bar on those allegations because it was the same issue, but I guess not responding is an admission of guilt. I was still reeling from my suspension, contacting the 500 active clients I had, trying to overcome my health problems, and contacting other lawyers to take my cases, which I was also require to do. The Bar had the suspension over me, plus my ex-wife had me arrested for her self sustained injuries and that didn't look good, either. I think I was pretty drained by the time of my hearing, but as an immigration lawyer, I specialized in hopeless cases, just the way I like them, because I thought I can win them, anyway. So I thought I would win this too. I thought everything was self evident, but the Bar wanted me out of there by hook or crook.

A few things seemed weird at the hearing. One, my clients said they didn't know they were filing for asylum. Maybe because it's a legal term or it had been over a year or more since I discussed their case with them, so they may have forgotten. But the weirdest part was that the receipts, which were part of the evidence, I gave my clients said asylum or I-589 (asylum's form number) on them. I guess that didn't matter, and I think the referee/judge thought Mexicans couldn't get asylum, either. He actually put that in the decision to disbar me when he stated I tried to put forth unwarranted claims. Because he had that attitude and didn't know the law, how can he decide accurately, more less judge. I had some of my staff members testify for me that our interviews were all the same, because they also interpreted for me. We averaged around five consultations a day; consequently, so my staff couldn't remember the people specifically; subsequently, (my referee/judge) determined since my staff didn't remember all the clients specifically, their testimony was inadmissible. I thought he might know the Rules of Evidence, where if evidence/behavior is part of a pattern, routine, or habit it is admissible, but not for me.

On the other hand, because the people with complaints against me remembered me, their testimony was admissible. Now it's not my word against their word, it's just their word against me. He also complained that I wasn't remorseful. If I thought I did something wrong maybe I would be remorseful. Is there an unspoken rule, to at least mandatorily seek mercy through remorse, for your innocents? And the meaning of frivolous, which is a legal term with its own definition is just the truth. Not something that was uselessly pursued. My Judge/Referee was unaware of the legal definition of "frivolous"; consequently, he determined my efforts were uselessly pursued.

I was going to skip my disbarment opinion because it basically reads like my decider/judge/referee was trying to convince himself to hide his ignorance, or was just plain delusional. The only thing that he said that was the truth was that I did not charge much. Of course, that made the other lawyers mad, concerned, and/or jealous. I had worked construction. I will not take advantage of my clients or anyone, that was barely making it by modest means, and busting their tail, everyday. The people I represented barely made over minimum wage. Charging them like my colleagues would be deceitful and dishonest. I have to live with my conscious. The amount other lawyers made our poor clients pay, was theft, or at a minimum, criminal. My goal always was to help the unrepresented and underrepresented. That is why I represented over 90% of all the immigration local clients. Other lawyers would tell me to stay out of their territory or charge more. I thought they were crazy on both counts. That's why Jim Fellows and I started the UNA Legal Clinic and the Public Interest Law Forum. I will feel better helping someone than being a millionaire. Now to the fun stuff.

According to the Referee, my efforts to help our new immigrants, was a scheme. Of course, that word gives it negative connotations. That word should be used for the bankers and Wall Street, not for someone trying to help the least fortunate. Evidently, trying to help those in need is a scheme. My scheme evidently was to use procedural manipulations to assist my client by using asylum as a vehicle to present other forms of relief for my clients. He stated that's not creative lawyering, it's deceitful and dishonest. It's really not none of the above. It was something I had been doing for years. I am sure the government or it's lawyers would have call me on that before, if it was deceitful or dishonest. In case he reads this, it is really okay to apply for more than one form of relief and one can actually withdraw any application at any time. For example, if you have a pending asylum case and your client gets married to an U.S. Citizen then it would be prudent and practical to withdrawal the asylum case, because the adjustment to a U.S. Citizen is generally, for sure. Or you can also argue your asylum case as well. Asylum cases actually are works in progress up until the individual hearing date (trial). Or maybe the judges just treated me more special then him while we practiced law, so he was unaware of that? He goes on to say that I had intentions of neglecting my cases or not following through. All 12 years of practicing immigration law I never neglected a case or never not followed through a case. I am not sure where he came up with that assumption, but I wasn't planning on changing the way I'd always done things over the years. That's why I had 90% of the immigration cases in Ashland. I never neglected a case and always followed through. After my back surgery I did take a couple weeks off and I had continuances that were all granted so I'm not sure if that's what he's talking about when I didn't go to court. Actually, I waited two years before I got the back surgery because I was worried about my clients. If one has their continuances granted there are no legal ramifications. Actually, getting a continuance granted is advantages in immigration law because, one, that gives them more time here with legal status with there work permit; and two, with time Congress may actually enact some type of legislation to help our newly arrived immigrants. I can tell by his reasoning he did not know immigration law. Ironically his reasoning, appeared to make it look like he cared and made it look like I didn't care or didn't know. So I'm giving him the benefit of the doubt that he had good intentions. Even the Nebraska Supreme Court didn't understand immigration, otherwise, they would have recognized the flaws in his legal reason. It's understandable because I was down in the trenches day after day, studying, practicing, and always asking questions. I always knew what I was doing because that was my job and my primary goal, to represent my clients the best I could. That means making mistakes but also learning from them, something my referee didn't have an opportunity to do. It's somewhat comical that he's concerned about Homeland Security's caseload, as he states in his decision against me. Homeland Security has billions and billions of dollars to work with and a staff of thousands. I had a little office with the staff of secretaries and a couple paralegals. What that actually says is they do not want to work. I know because my office was right next-door to their office. They left at 4:30 or five every day, I left at 10 or midnight every day. It's still funny that I had the ability to take that agency down. Best way to stop that, get rid of me. My Judge knew that all my clients were subject to deportation anyway. It is obvious he would rather have them in that situation then to be proactive like I was and actually try to help them. He knew all the other lawyers wouldn't help them (primarily because they needed to keep their employer happy - The Bar) and once I was out of the picture they are out of the country. He was doing his justice to me and leaving all the people I was trying to help with no hope. He had to realize that, unless he was willing to help them. If he knew enough about immigration he actually could have. I talked to an immigration lawyer about the correct procedures to help them despite my disbarment. He agreed, but did nothing, I think he was afraid. They already used me for the example of not making Homeland Security to busy or legally helping the wrong people. All the DRs (Disciplinary Rules in the Attorneys Code of Ethics) he said I violated, shows his ignorance even more. Somewhat of a comedy of errors. He said since I asked for the money I earned, I was practicing law. He should be aware that a disbarred or suspended lawyer is still entitled to the money they made up to that point. I guess I was special because I had to return all the money I made, even the money I made before my suspension. Besides that, that makes the Bar even look more righteous. Anyone can fill out forms for anyone in this country. Again they put me on a pedestal because I was the exception, I couldn't even fill out forms. Anyone can take pictures for passports, but again, I'm special because I was not allowed to take pictures either. I'm glad I didn't tell them

I use White Cloud tissue paper, they would've made me switch to Charmin, I'm sure. I'm so glad I didn't become their puppet. Homeland Security wanted me to be a lawyer for them. That would be too hard for me because I think people are humans, not cattle. You know animals to be herded off to the slaughter! And now it looks like it doesn't matters if they are children or not. Especially, Mexican children who are treated harsher than other children, under the current law signed by President Bush. As we are witnessing now. And it appears that the government would rather put those children in concentration camps than treat them humanly, according to the law. Too many dark skinned children, time to manipulate the law to excluded them too. Sorry, I got to live with myself and look at myself. My skin might be brown but I'm no brown noser. I'm pretty sure this is how the persecution of the Jews started. Looks kind of innocent at first but then before you know it. I wasn't too concerned about my popularity. I skipped most or all of the Bar events and never went shopping to give the judges Christmas gifts, as other lawyers did. Give me a break I had a job to do, I didn't have time for all that and what little time I had, I tried to spend with my family. My judge also claimed my claims have no merit. And he was going to make sure they never did. My problem is I'm colorblind and I look at all of us as humanity. People are generally good but when you throw hate at them, what do you expect? I'm just glad that he wasn't a judge when our country made decisions on women's rights and civil rights. I'm not saying this to demean him I'm saying this to try to understand. If he knew immigration law, he had to know disbarring me would immediately throw all my clients into deportation and my strategy would have kept them here for at least five or six years. Furthermore, he knows in immigration law, an immigrant has to subject themselves to deportation to argue their case and have any relief from being deported. In other words, they are guilty until they prove their innocence, not the other way around. I needed an impartial immigration judge, with full knowledge of immigration law, to make the decision. Someone that knew the law. I guess it's all good, the system needs sheep not advocates. Judge Queries determination that the applications were frivolous was overturned on appeal by a higher court; obviously, he didn't know the law either. I guess I should've told him but he's the Judge, I figured he should knew. At least, his superiors knew. I wonder if he knew that, but schemed to stop me and my clients, to lessen Homeland Security's caseload, or if he really was that ignorant. I just figured as lawyers we need to know how words are defined in the legal sense. At the time, I didn't know he was going to say the applications were frivolous, otherwise I would've showed him what frivolous meant. I believe if the lawyers would have been more vigilant and proactive in Nazi Germany the holocaust could have been avoided. You know, there goes the neighborhood. In hindsight, I may have done more to protect myself from their attacks; but I have a feeling, even if I had my clients sign everything in their blood it would not had made a difference.

I was getting pretty sick about this time due to my to my declining health. My job was done, my ex-wife wouldn't let me see my kids so the marriage was done. I got sentenced for 90 days in Sarpy County due my ex- wife's lying to the police that I injured her, from her self inflicted injuries. I lost all my possessions. I didn't even have a car or anywhere to live. While in jail, my ex took everything I worked for, hid it in a storage and filed for divorce. So much for the plan of using all my money to pay for her bills, then live together in our other house. So my health, family and livelihood were all gone, but, eerily I felt at peace. What's that saying, if you have nothing you have nothing to lose?Or me with some delusional thinking, even when your backs in the gutter, you can still gaze at the stars!

While staying in my sister's house, a reporter from the nearby state, Brianna Blake, called me and asked for an interview and told me that the "government" had promised the people who testified against me their "papers", but instead deported them after my disbarment. I told her I would give her the interview, but wanted her to put what she told me in the article. She agreed. I would have probably talked to her anyway. I was kind of held up anyway, wondering if I could ever walk again. I was able to walk again in about a year. Ms. Blake told me she would send me the article. She did send it, but I didn't see nothing about my clients who back stabbed me and were double crossed. It's no wonder. You get what you get, when you deal with the anti-Christ. Anyway, she told me that her editor wouldn't let her put that in the article, so that was that. In the back of my mind, however, I knew if I could get her to tell the truth to the right people I might get vindicated. Since then I have hired thee private investigators and two or three lawyers who couldn't find her. It's like she has dropped off the face of the earth. Maybe, I should look at the Obituaries or the Witness Protection Program. Just when you think it won't get any worse.

CHAPTER SIX

The End

All that I've talked about happened around 2004. The same day my house got repossessed I was taken by ambulance to the hospital. Blood clots and kidney failure. Five days in ICU and I thought I died. And I really felt like I could accept it. I think I might have been at the point where the certainty of the near future was worst than the unknown. You know, I saw the light and all the clouds in front of the light and it didn't seem so bad. I was really cold, like 20 below cold, but I felt like I was at peace. But then I remembered my parents said that bad things never die. I'm joking all you haters. Actually, I was thinking what I always thought, God won't put anything in front of me that I can't handle. Plus, I was always really blessed and seemed to be lucky. I also figured I was being tested and when that happens I was like, throw it at me, I can do it. I spent a few months back-and-forth in the hospital. Just about the time I was getting out of the hospital again, it was time to go to trial for my ex-wife falsely accusing me of assault. Of course the jury believed her lies, the big bad Mexican had to hit that little, "innocent" girl.

She was very crafty and I think if she ever needs to switch careers she would be a great actress. Nonetheless, jail gave me a place to live. It was funny, they put handcuffs on my walker and attached them to me. Believe me, if I could walk I might have tried to get away. I'm kidding. After I got out of jail, it took me about a year to walk again. I felt so fortunate just to be able to walk. And I look at disabled people a lot different after that. I was also fortunate, that my sister let me stay in her spare bedroom, while I recovered. I finally was able to go back to school working on a chemistry degree, but ran out of financial aid and couldn't qualify for a private loan, so I didn't quite get enough hours to complete the degree. Financial aid was limited because I had a degree already. I was able to get an apartment around 2005. And then around 2006 I had some interesting visitors. An IRS agent and a Homeland Security investigator. I let them in my apartment because I didn't have nothing to hide. They were nice at first and I was telling the truth about everything but then they became somewhat aggressive. A interrogation tactic. I forgot the truth is what got me in trouble in the first place. They accursed me of hiding money in the Cayman Islands, Switzerland or in my mattress. I told them if I had money like that I wouldn't be living in some shabby apartment. They still wanted to see me later. If I had the money they thought I had, I wouldn't be staying in here. A week later, I was indicted for money laundering and mail fraud. Eight to ten years.

Perfect. Trying to get my life together. Why keep things simple? I felt comfortable, just like I felt before I went to my disciplinary hearing. Then I felt my heart sink to my feet. What the shuck; they already took everything I had, but that wasn't good enough? Now they want my freedom. Oh well, the Mexicans rule in the Pen and I'd have plenty of time to become a Chess Master. I've been playing tournament chess since I was 16. Now I can accomplish that goal! Plus, I would be a great jailhouse lawyer; consequently, I would pick up some extra commissary money. I learned a lot my 67 days in jail. What are they going to do now if I practice without a license in the pen? Take my law degree and throw me in jail? LOL!

I fully cooperated with the U.S. Attorney's Office, primarily for the same reason. I thought that the truth will prevail, even if the justice system I tried to defend all those years was consistently knocking me down. I guess I was suppose to be scared because they offered me a year in the pen, if I lied to them and said I was guilty, by plea bargaining. I told my lawyer, Mr. Micheal Tasset, to tell them to stick it. In the event that we win, which is unlikely, because they have a 99% conviction rate, they stated they would refile the charges? I told Mr. Tasset, good, we'll beat those charges too. They got some nerve, trying to make me lie about something I didn't do. I didn't have a lot, but I will not allow them to take away what little dignity I had left. I'd rather be a political prisoner than lie to myself and them, to make their job easy. They should know by now that if I can't out smart them, I could sure outwork them. I was getting a little upset about being under constant surveillance, too. First, from my Bar Trustee, now the judicial injustice system too! Always explaining what I was doing for years for trying to help our second class, slave, citizens who basically have no rights and are constantly threatened. I always told my clients, your rights stopped when you made it across the border. Five years of surveillance, maybe I should've ran for the border, too.

CHAPTER SEVEN

The End Of The End

For two years, Mr. Micheal Tasset and I planned for the case. After months and months of trying to teach Mr. Tasset Immigration Law, he finally concluded, "there is a method to the madness." He also told me at one point, "Clemente, you have probably forgotten more about immigration law than most people remember." The reason he said that is because we used the governments expert witnesses to win the case. I remember the last day of testimony I feel asleep during a break, I was so confident. If I go to the Pen, by chess rating would go through the sky! If I win maybe the government would have additional time to focus on real criminals, like those who took the economy down with fake documents. No not "illegals" with fake documents, bankers, lawyers, and Wall Street with fake useless documents they made up to scheme millions of people out of there life savings! I keep forgetting - there is law and there is justice - two different things. How silly of me!

Again, the government's defense was a comedy of errors. The indictment said Mexicans are not eligible asylum, yet

Mr. Tasset used Homeland Security's own data, proving Mexicans are routinely granted asylum. They brought in "experts" from Chicago and Washington D.C. who helped us. They brought in about ten moving boxes of all my bank records for ten years or more to prove I laundered money. They must have spent at least $100,000.00 in tax payers money, in their efforts to throw me in the pen. But as Mike argued, if the mail fraud is not proven then the money laundering charge, must fall too. Everyday of the week long case gave us more and more hope; but I had always believed the truth was my best defense and saw what that got me so far, so I was preparing myself for prison. I watched every prison movie I could and dreamed of becoming a chess master. I also began trying to enjoy each day a little more knowing this could be the last few days of my freedom. I also learned at the trial they had me under constant surveillance, probably afraid I might try to help an immigrant. The landlord who locked up my office due to nonpayment eventually gave me one day to get what was left in my office. Or I should say what was left of it, after everyone had picked through what they wanted. I found one of my passport cameras and thought I would try to make some money taking some passport pictures, but was told to stop. Remember I was constantly under surveillance. Our tax dollars at work!

Boss, who owned one of the local Spanish Newspapers came to my trial and wrote an article, after I told him if the truth comes out I will win, he wrote in his newspaper that I thought I would win, but he doubted it, because the Bar Association already made a decision and that was that. I had given him an interview after my suspension and tried to tell him this story so I might get some support. To make a long story short, he just talked about how depressed I was because that was the focus of his questions. I told him I wasn't exactly happy and maybe a little depressed, but I was primarily working on getting my health back. Anyway, the article stated I was depressed, but just think how depressed my former deported clients are. So much for support, now the Latino community was against me, too. I asked him why he never mentioned my motives to help and that the people who testified against me got deported. He told me if I didn't like the article to start my own newspaper. Now I know why his self serving paper went out of business.

In the preparation of the trial, Homeland Security, gave us access to all the alleged frivolous filings and lo and behold we found Judge Queries erroneous decision. His decision that the applications were frivolous was overturned, and that was one of the main reason for my disbarment. I wanted to testify at my trial, but Mike told me the government witnesses already testified for me, which was true. But the main reason I won the case, in my assessment, was the testimony of my life long friend, Yolanda Garcia Ramos. After her testimony I was mesmerized. I was sure I would win the Chicano, Hispanic, and Latino (CHL) person of a lifetime award. I never knew anyone thought of me like that. Growing up, finally realizing I was one and/or all those persons in the categories, CHL, I thought something was intrinsically wrong with the way minorities and women were treated and thought, instead of complaining to do something. So if there was a protest or concern I volunteered to do my part. Yolanda told the Judge and reminded me of when I would protest for equal civil rights. She stated and I paraphrase, "I wasn't quite sure what he was doing, but I'd see him out there demonstrating for some cause." I joined the all the CHL clubs in my early years at the University of Nantucket at Ashland (UNA), during my time there in the early seventies. I had good mentors such as Virgil Armaderaz, Pat McKee, Rodger Ramirez, Tculadal (a CHL who changed his name to an Aztec warrior), Ramon Hernandez, and others. I also learned from my Goodyear Scholarship Professor who tried to instill some confidence in me by saying people want to know what I had to say and I was born to succeed. Things I never heard before. I had gotten used to hearing being Mexican was a strike against you, not being accepted for being a Mexican, my opportunities are limited for being a Mexican, not much of a chance for being a Mexican, and experiencing situations that appeared to make that seem true. The only difference is that I knew I had will power and determination, but wasn't sure how to get where I wanted to go against the opinions of others. Yolanda was the first female Executive Director over the once called Chicano Center. Her list of accomplishments spanned over decades and as she spoke I saw the connection between her and U.S. District Court Judge Spark, who was one of the first woman to become a United States District Court Judge. Remember, I was the guy who didn't know I was Mexican until twelve when my classmates made it so real. I was the guy who thought Spanish wasn't worth learning. I was the person with Mexican ancestors who was totally assimilated who was alienated from most most Mexicans due to a language barrier and a lot of white society for being Mexican. Growing up the latter part of my childhood in a military family, I realized even though

I was categorized as part of the CHL race, I was really just part of the human race, color blind and loving everyone as human beings. That is what really got me. How and why people are against each other because of different DNA and pigmentation and what I could do to stop it, I had to try. I would of helped anyone that was being treated unjustly even if I had to go down with them. I thank God for giving me the opportunity. I waited a year for the decision but finally in December 2008, I could finally breath. It's 2014 now. With good time I would be getting out about now. If nothing else, it helped me appreciate every day, knowing I was on borrowed time, if justice had not prevailed, again.

In closing, immigrants, like all our ancestors, made America. It was easy for our ancestors to come, but for some reason, the United States has lost its willingness to help refugees and those with high ideals about the American Dream. We are all God's children. To deny others is to deny ourselves. God help us!

Epilogue

This book is based on a true story but not a book trying to further my political agenda. If anything, I prefer to be independent and I appreciate thoughtful opinions, of all kinds, that are not hateful to our fellow spirits. "I believe in the idea of amnesty for those who have put down roots and have lived here even though some time back they may have entered here illegally". Ronald Reagan. We only have two viable alternatives to choose the way our system is set up and Reagan and Lincoln (both Republicans) were champions for civil rights and humanity.

Growing up totally assimilated it took me a while to realize I was considered different and that fact thrusted me into hurtful situations. I was going to say, the more things change the more they stay the same when it comes to race relations; but no good deeds goes unpunished, may be more appropriate. As a brown person, besides being pulled over for nothing, called racial slurs, rejected by girls and their parents for being a certain race, not encouraged by my high school counselor, police lying to a judge in court about me, working in the lettuce fields in California when I was 13, being the first Chicano in a labor union where the population of the city's Latinos was and is 40%, threatened to be beaten up for being of Mexican descent, being disbarred in the only state that won't give our "Dreamers" (children brought by their parents that where born in Mexico or other country) a license to drive, and where minority attorneys are more likely to be disciplined then their white counterparts, all is well. Because I don't have to pay for a tan. Why do people pay to look like me then reject me, and others, with the same physical characteristics? Okay I was a little facetious the last two sentences, but, clearly, because we classify ourselves as groups, we divide ourselves. As an American with Mexican ancestors, I feel those persecuted spirits' pain, not because I have to go through their misery, but only that my little experiences with racial profiling and discrimination are only a small reminder and are nothing compared to the hate and rejection they must feel. But even if these people were disabled and diseased with purple spots they are still God's creations.

All is well. We are all God's children. All in this together, with the same God who has different names around the world. When we ignore the misery and perpetuate the stereotype of any group, the misery does not go away and we hurt the humanity that we are all part of. It also raises the risk, that hate begets more hate. With spirituality every problem has a solution. We are encouraged to tell the truth, so as in life, most things are paradoxically, and obviously telling the truth, as in the case of my clients, did not work. I should be upset if what Brianna told me was the truth, because that would mean my clients sacrificed me for a chance to be here legally, and in the process they also became the sacrificial lamb. However, I have learned love and forgiveness and choosing peace over revenge, hate, or regret always wins out. I also realize desperate people do desperate things. When we deal with men's laws, justice and the law are surely not one in the same. That is what they probably meant in law school. I can not imagine God dividing up the earth and telling us to fight for every inch of it. We are spiritual mirrors of each other, with the divine right to travel with no borders. But our ego (edging out God), is suspicious at best and vicious at worse. With all the money spent on border control we could train, educate, and incorporate our newest immigrants easily. People always say we can not help everyone when we are one in the same. To not help is a crime against humanity. We throw away enough food to feed everyone in the world. I read somewhere, where a USC asked a young girl in Africa why she would like to come here and she said, "Because even the poor people are fat!"

I am not convinced God plays favorites, only the ego could do that! But with a combined Spiritual consciousness we can and will defeat those things called discrimination, prejudice, alienation, and exclusion of any of our fellow spirits and their divinity. I'm not saying we should have our Central American neighbors empty out their prisons and bring them here as the Europeans did. We need to protect all of God's children from further harm and we do not need any more people who will not respect God's gift of life that he has given all of us. I had to come with terms myself for living off the misery of a group of God's children, as an attorney, despite my good intentions. But I know my "Source" as a loving and forgiving God and I know to be forgiven I must forgive. That means I must love and forgive myself, and my enemies, as well.

Families of the human race all want their family members, at least in their lives, if nothing else. As mentioned, I did not want to hear about "family values" (something I don't hear much of, anymore). Mexico was a third of the United States, at one time and traveling back and forth was rather easy so naturally there are family here and family there. Mexico has historical been used for labor during good economic times and during the bad times we have witnessed what happen, for example the "Great Deportation" during the Great Depression. Little regard has been given to our fellow humans hopes, dreams, or even something simple that we take for granted like being by their family members.

I know there is a debate about abortion and a woman's right to choose. You have probably figured out that I am pro-life; however, I am also pro women's rights, especially after witnessing their struggle to be recognized and counted, somewhat like our old, new immigrants, human beings, and inhabitants. The Founding Fathers even recognized "All men are created equal." It is intellectually inconsistent, logically dishonest, and morally incapable to be pro-life and anti-immigrant. Our Creator recognizes that life is from the womb to the tomb. We know that life should be cared for before birth and not forgotten after birth. I feel a moral obligation for myself, God, and mankind to stop our fellow spirits from dying in the dessert, innocent children turned away for further suffering and possible death, families' separated, deported, incarcerated for trying to see ones spouse or children, subjected to a system where one is considered a criminal alien, yet not even given any rights we afford criminals, and the list goes on. If that was the case I would be pro-pre-birth not pro life. We help countries half way across the world to protect refugees, yet, turn our refugees away. That is un-American and a crime against humanity, especially when we are so blessed. That was my limit. I try not to cry. I can't even imagine in my worse nightmares what it is like for our innocent blessings, on the border, to be treated worst than we treat our animals. I have a dream too. My dream is to go to the border and help, so help me God. My dream is that the ideals that our country lives by - that we are all created equal, inside and outside our man made borders. And I have a dream that no book will ever have to be written like this again.

All we need is empathy and love in our hearts, instead of greed, suppression, and the love for money in our policies and to practice what Jesus taught us. The greatest commandment is that we shall love God with all our heart, with all our soul and all our mind. And the second commandant is like it; "Though shall love thy neighbor as thyself. On these two commandments hang all the ***LAW*** and the prophets". As the Native Americans reminded us: No tree has branches so foolish as to fight among themselves.

Printed in the United States
By Bookmasters